About the Author

Amber Deckers grew up in South Africa where she studied film, before going on to work for an advertising agency. During this time, she was a part-time journalism student and eventually joined *Marie Claire* as a features and fashion writer and book reviewer.

Deciding to swap the shores of Africa for London, Amber worked for various publishers in London before joining an independent film production company with the idea of creating a television programme about teenage issues. When the project was shelved, Amber decided to put her research and ideas into a novel, which became *Ella Mental and the Good Sense Guide*, published by Orchard in 2005. The sequel, *Ella Mental – Life, Love and More Good Sense*, followed in 2006.

Amber and her husband, Craig, have recently returned to the UK after living in Grenada. They now live in Surrey with their son, Tay, and Blue and Calypso – both rescue animals from the West Indies. Amber currently works as a freelance journalist whilst also writing her next book about the wonderful Liberty Belle.

For Mum

ORCHARD BOOKS
338 Euston Road, London NW1 3BH
Orchard Books Australia
Level 17/207 Kent Street, Sydney, 2000, NSW, Australia

ISBN: 978 1 84362 728 9

First published in Great Britain in 2007
A paperback original
Text © Amber Deckers 2007
The right of Amber Deckers to be identified as the author of
this work has been asserted by her in accordance with the
Copyright, Designs and Patents Act, 1988.
A CIP catalogue record for this book is available from the
British Library.

1 3 5 7 9 10 8 6 4 2
Printed in Great Britain

Orchard Books is a division of Hachette Children's Books
www.orchardbooks.co.uk

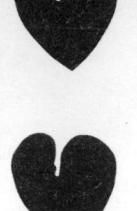

Amber Deckers

Liberty Belle I Love You, Goodbye

ORCHARD BOOKS

Part One
The End

one
when all is said and done

I don't know what's brought it on but lately I've started talking to myself. The good news is that these conversations usually take place in my head (and not out loud), because when I get going there's just no stopping me. I have absolutely no control over these talking thoughts whatsoever. My best bet is to ignore the voices and hope that I'll eventually bore myself into silence.

That's what I call them – talking thoughts, and these days I always seem to have a voice in my head nattering on about everything and nothing in particular. I just ramble on and on and on. You'd think that I'd eventually run out of opinions, but I don't. I just keep on going. And going. *Ah!* Someone's boring me, and I think it's me. What must a girl do to get some peace and quiet around here? I've tried emptying my head entirely and focusing on thinking about nothing at all, but I usually just end up talking myself through the whole process and defeating the object entirely. It's a vicious circle. The part of my brain that's a busybody is obviously not communicating with the rest of my brain that just wants some peaceful silence.

Sometimes the devil jumps inside my head and turns my talking thoughts nasty. I might be walking along the high street and see a newborn baby and compare it to a dimpled alien; or I may get stuck behind a granny pushing a shopping trolley and, in my irritation, mentally banish the old dear to a comfortable retirement home where she doesn't need to shop for groceries and get in the way of young people like me who have things to buy and people to see. Once I passed a drunken man on a street corner slurring for small change, but instead of showing kindness my talking thoughts just blurted out, 'You'll only spend my pocket money on booze, so forget it buddy!' I know it's wrong and mean and not very compassionate at all, but I can't help it. My talking thoughts have a mind of their own. Or maybe I'm just not a very nice girl.

Right now I'm slumped in my seat and staring at the fleshy boy-man who is sitting across from me and staring out of the murky train window. There's really not much else to do on a train except stare. The boy-man's eyes are deep and round and outlined by glasses and his hair looks slippery and stand-up wild. His face is still creased from napping but he's wide awake and suddenly pointing enthusiastically at the passing scenery with his left pinkie finger. Who in their right mind points with their pinkie finger? my talking thoughts gripe. Everybody knows that's what the pointing finger is for. That's how it got its name, for crying out loud. And hello, they're *just cows*.

I'm too easily irritated, that's my problem – and I blame it on all those teenage hormones whizzing around my system like it's the final lap of the Grand Prix. The fact that my life is as significant as a bowl of mushy peas could also have something to do with it. I was a much nicer person when my life didn't suck.

A balding train conductor has just emerged through the concertina doors, pushing a tiered trolley that's no doubt stacked with warm cans of fizzy, cold tea, meat-flavoured crisps, soggy sandwiches and biscuits with clusters that are definitely not chocolate or anything the FSA (FYI: Food Standards Agency) would approve of. A few passengers, desperate to fill a gap and some time, are reaching up with their hands and yoo-hoo-wiggling their fingers in the air, but the majority are content to continue snoozing or staring or doing whatever it was they were doing before the man, his shiny head and the trolley, made an entrance.

I make a bet with myself that Pinkie-Pointer will

have something from the trolley. He's enjoying this trip too much not to. The conductor pulls up at our row and raises his eyebrows up at me questioningly. I quickly slouch down further in my seat and pretend to sleep, although I'm really spying on you-know-who sitting across from me through the narrow slit in my eyelids. Pinkie-Pointer is too excited to wait for his own personal eyebrow invitation from the conductor.

'You wouldn't have any pink sugar-coated almonds, would you?' he asks in a breathy voice, jabbing his left pinkie in the direction of the trolley. Somebody has confused this train trip to Brighton with a wedding, it seems.

'If it ain't on the trolley then we don't have it, mate,' the conductor explains with a patient sigh.

'Oh right,' Pinkie-Pointer groans. 'Well, let's see what you do have then.' He stretches his spine to get a better view of the trolley's contents. 'Crisps um, nooo,' he considers thoughtfully, tapping at the foil packets with his you-know-what. 'A sandwich...biscuits?' Two taps. 'No, I don't think so. I really could do with some sugar. Are you quite sure you don't have any sugared almonds? Any colour will do.'

'I'm quite sure,' the conductor exhales. 'Now wha'ilibe?'

Pinkie-Pointer lifts a small carton filled with banana

milkshake from the trolley and inspects the ingredients printed on the side, underlining the writing with the smallest finger on his right hand. Perhaps the left one's grown tired. 'Right, here you go then,' he finally pips, extracting a pound coin from his corduroy pocket and handing it over to the visibly relieved conductor who very quickly pops it into his money bag and resumes his trip down the aisle.

My eyes are still slits but I watch carefully as my strange neighbour discards the straw glued to the carton's side and punctures the small circle of foil at the top with his front tooth. He then begins gently massaging the carton's sides while simultaneously attempting to mop at the bubbling yellow fountain with his outstretched tongue. This kind of thing always happens to me. Either there are a lot of weirdos about, or I'm weirdo flypaper, my talking thoughts bleat dismally. Although I am the one talking to myself, so maybe I'm really the weirdo and I just don't know it. That's the upside to being a weirdo, I suppose. You think everybody else is loopy and you're the sane one.

Suddenly I feel something heavy on me. Is somebody scrutinising the scrutiniser? I lift my gaze and my eyes collide with the scruffy skateboarder sitting across the aisle from me. His striped boxer shorts are sticking out of his jeans which are so baggy they look like a skirt. His hair is gelled as stiff and straight as razor wire; he looks like a cartoon who's just had a big fright.

'Creepazoid!' I mutter softly and throw him my best just-sucked-on-a-lemon scowl. I hate being looked at. I then quickly raise the open black notebook resting on my lap to my face like a shield. Keep your greasy eyeballs to yourself, Skater Boy, I fume inwardly and peer at my handwriting on the page that's now just an inch or two from my nose. Top centre of the lined sheet of paper is the heading: MY DYING TO DO LIST. To date the list only consists of four numbered points, and the first item on the list is: 'Select a burial outfit'. So there's no Nobel Prize for guessing that this is not a rosy list of things I'm dying to do, but rather a list of things I must do before I die. Or pass on. Or kick the bucket. Or head off for the big sleep. People do like to dress it up.

The fact that this notebook is black is no coincidence. It's the colour of death, or in my culture it is anyway. I'm talking sayonara marinara. See you at the pearly gate, mate. My birth certificate is about to expire and there's no point in getting soppy or sentimental about it. Of course I realise that we're all going to die one day. This is different. I know I'm going to be worm food one day *soon*. I suppose in a way I'm luckier than

12

most. Even if I don't know how or exactly what day and time it's going to happen, I know it's not far off. At least I can be prepared. I'm getting my personal business in order, and these days I only ever go out in my good underwear. That's point number four on My Dying To Do List: no more comfy balloon pants with holes or stretched elastic.

Of course I don't have shatterproof evidence that I'm going to die soon; it's just something I know – like when I *just knew* that Skater Boy was staring at me. Humans are animals after all, we can sense things and we have instincts. I suppose I'm just more in tune with mine than most thirteen year olds. Up until about two months ago I'd never really given dying much thought. The whole notion crept up on me one night while I was lying in bed and waiting for sleep. I often think mad thoughts when I'm lying alone in bed at night in the dark, but this time it was different. This time I was completely and utterly consumed by the conviction that one day – and one day soon – I simply wasn't going to exist any more. It wasn't the fact that I might choke on a chicken bone or trip on my shoelace and get squished by the school bus; it wasn't *how* I was going to die that overwhelmed me. What kept me awake at night was the fact that the rest of the world would continue living and going about its business and very little would change without me around. People would barely even notice that I'd vacated the planet. Sure, the shoes in my cupboard would sprout cobwebs, my toothbrush would turn mouldy and my CDs would gather dust, but other than that – what would really change? My classroom seat would quickly be filled by another (prettier, smarter and more popular) girl, my father and Misty would have their new baby, and Mum would buy a healing crystal and learn a new chant to see her through the loss of her only child. Years would become decades and who would really care that Liberty Belle once breathed and gave her best? Sort of. Well, sometimes.

Since that night I've been thinking non-stop about death – or about my own death in particular, I should say. I don't make a conscious effort to think about it. It's just something that's sitting and waiting for me on the front porch of my brain, so it must be an omen. The universe is sending me a message and I intend to make these last few weeks or months or whatever time I have left on this earth count for something.

Since my parents' divorce, planning my departure is just about the only thing I do still have some control over. Come to think of it, my parents have a lot to answer for. Their divorce has made my life a smouldering sulphur-pit of hell. Mind you, their marriage made my life a smouldering sulphur-pit of hell too. Of course I realise that in this day and age it's more common for parents to divorce than to give that 'until death do us part' oath a second thought – so I'm not copping for the sympathy plea, but my parents have openly disliked one another since I was three (which is as far back as I can remember, so it's probably been longer). My parents have zilch in common. My father is a rigid control freak and my mum is a hippy Mother Earth worshipping freak. How they ever came to be at the same party in the same university halls is anybody's guess, and either nobody told them or they temporarily forgot how babies were made (I've heard hormones can do that to you), but one fumble in the dark turned into twelve long years.

When Mum found out she was pregnant they sat down and agreed to get married. They thought it was the right thing to do. Plan A was to try very hard to be a happy family, and Plan B was to live under one roof until I was at least twelve years old (insert some misguided notion about a stable childhood here). They thought they owed me that much. How they figured their break-up would be less traumatic if they timed it to coincide with the onset of my adolescence I'll never know, but that was probably about the last thing my parents ever agreed on. From that day, whenever things became a little tense between the two of them (just breathing could set the other one off), either Mum would remind my father that the only reason she hadn't left was because of me, or else my father would be the one doing the reminding. That piece of information would have worked so much better as their little secret, I always thought.

For my parents, the final year of their marriage was like the lead-up to some exciting expedition, one that required a lot of planning and forethought. My father put our house on the market and started moving his stuff in with Misty (his very *personal* fitness trainer). He had already rerouted his post to her home address a few weeks earlier, and I'd been measured up for my ruffled shimmering-fungus bridesmaid's dress before the ink on the divorce papers was even dry.

Mum, meanwhile, planned spiritual retreats and spoke loudly about 'finally following her calling' – usually throwing the phrase 'spiritually constipated pencil-neck' somewhere into the same sentence. Mum's calling turned out to be a New Age commune in Brighton, which – if you don't count delays – is only a *five hour* train journey from Manchester, which is where I'm forced to co-exist with my father and his very pregnant personal fitness trainer. I mean girlfriend. I mean wife. My twelfth birthday was a day of great celebration in our house.

two
nice to see you too

I slump and wait and watch to make sure that Pinkie-Pointer and Skater Boy have left the train and disappeared from the platform before I even attempt to drag my backpack down the aisle. I want to avoid those two – for mental and personal health reasons. By the time I reach the open train doors the platform has almost cleared, but I can't spot Mum anywhere. And my mum's easy to spot, so she's obviously late. Again.

There's no Big Giant Voice reminding me to 'mind the gap' today either, but I make a point of doing so anyway. I don't want to die before I've seen my mum. Not that there's any hurry. I'm perched on my backpack and nibbling on my bottom lip for a tedious twenty minutes before I eventually spy her soaring along the deserted platform trailing a blur of flowing tie-dyed cotton and clunking multi-coloured bead chains. I know she knows I've seen her, but I don't budge a muscle until she's finally standing, panting and gasping for breath, right in front of me. It's just as well I was the last one off the train because not only is she very late, but she's bleached her short boy hair as white as a goose. I thought teenagers – not mums – were supposed to have the identity crisis.

'Libby Bellie!' she gushes and flings her arms expectantly open. I really wish she wouldn't call me that. I sound like a fat, naked Buddha.

'Hello Mother,' I sigh and roll my eyes to the back of my head like marbles. We only have two days together; I can't believe she'd waste a single minute of this time. 'Where were you?' I whine.

'I'm so sorry darling, I got caught up,' is her excuse. 'I've been doing volunteer work at the Centre for Sumskiri Khuki.' Are we still speaking English? my talking thoughts wonder.

'It means the centre for spiritual enlightenment,' she reads my mind.

'Yeah, well how about you do some volunteer work at the Centre for Liberty Belle!' I bark. 'And it's just Libby, can we drop the Bellie please.' Crikey, you'd think I was still seven.

'So sorry darling,' Mum croons and swallows me up in her arms. She grips me tightly and squeezes me to her chest and I close my eyes and press my ear to her heart and listen for its strong, rhythmic drumming. If I'm patient, her energy will flow into my veins and find its way to my core – and once again breathe life into my tired and gloomy overgrown heart. I could stand like this forever. This is how it was when I was growing inside her. Nothing could separate us then. It really has been forever. Her perfume is musky and I try to sniff through its veil and root out her real scent. I haven't forgotten the smell of her warm, early-morning skin when she would tiptoe into my bedroom and kiss my eyelids awake. That was a long time ago but Mum remembers how we were; the memories are making her body tremble too.

'Right, shall we get going then?' she finally murmurs and gently prises me from her chest. Her eyes are glistening but I pretend not to notice.

'Sure,' I reply and reach for my backpack, suddenly grateful to have something else to focus on.

'So how are you and how was your trip?' she asks as we negotiate our way to the car park. It's impossible to miss the metallic purple Alfa Romeo Mum's had for ever and takes great pride in calling Aurora (who was a Roman goddess). My father has a phobia for anything Italian – wine and engineering especially, which is precisely why Mum bought Aurora in the first place. Their mutual contempt made them predictable.

'I'm fine and it was fine,' I mumble without offering

any details. Pinkie-Pointer and Skater Boy weren't *that* interesting.

'And how are your father and Shifty?' Mum knows full well that my father's wife's name is Misty, but in spite of all her centred spirituality she still gets a huge amount of twisted pleasure out of calling her Shifty. 'She must be enormous by now, I should imagine,' she adds and purses her lips. She looks happily content, like she has a delicious sweet in her mouth – or knows something Misty and my father have yet to discover. Of course Mum swears that she doesn't give a flying soya bean that my father is remarried and about to become a parent for the second time. She also supposedly doesn't care that his new wife's toned and perfect figure made the cover of *Ms Fitness Magazine* not once but twice. She says that the only reason she dislikes Shifty is because of the 'principle of her actions' which – in normal speak – means that even if my parents did have a diabolical marriage, Misty still had no right getting involved with a man who was officially still married to the mother of his only child. 'She should have waited until you turned twelve,' Mum would fume, until one day I erupted and swore that if anyone in our family ever mentioned the number twelve again I would make a deliberate point of using *Crimewatch* as my personal dating agency. Well, it was the stirring of a rebellion anyway.

'So?' Mum asks.

'So what?' I mumble and blink my pupils back into focus. The dream-catcher dangling from the rear view mirror is swaying to and fro with the chugging of the car and it's strangely hypnotising.

'Your father? Shifty?' Mum reminds me.

'Oh, they're OK I guess,' I mutter indifferently. 'Dad is still as sergeant-major strict as ever. Misty is still as pregnant as ever. And all they ever do is talk about this baby they're going to have. Crap, the way they go on about it you'd think that they were the first people to ever have a flipping baby – like they just invented having babies, or something.'

'Don't say crap,' Mum orders as she negotiates the traffic ahead. 'It sounds very common, like people who wear skin-tight Spandex.' Mum relishes the small digs the most. 'How are you feeling about the baby, Lib? You're not feeling left out, are you?' Now she sounds more serious.

Am I feeling left out? my talking thoughts consider. Well, let's see: I suppose my father does take time out of his very busy schedule to remind me every single day that I'm about to become a big sister and so should therefore act accordingly (like I was put on this earth for the sole purpose of being a big sister). And by 'act accordingly' he means that I should keep better time, be neater, get better grades, always be within shouting distance but never in his face, stand straighter, dress better, be quiet and never ever question him. As for dear Misty, she really is too vacant to be mean and tolerates me like I'm a visiting relative who needs fresh towels and a ride into town every so often. She always looks surprised to see me and can never seem to remember very much about me – like whether I eat cauliflower or not, or where I go to school, or how old I am.

My father and I have never been close; I can't blame that on Misty. He's a discipline junkie who expects the entire world to fall in behind him. He and his new wife are bound by their mutual passion for repetitive exercise; Misty because – like a hamster on a wheel – she really does have a very fleeting short-term memory and is easily occupied, and my father because it'll make him a lean, mean machine. I don't know if he's head-over-heels for Misty, all I know is that he found the exact opposite of my mum and went and married her. Mum is a vegetarian environmentalist who is concerned with peace and enlightenment; Misty never leaves the house without her lipstick and Lycra and her main concern is improving her muscle-to-fat ratio. Even if I did feel left out, I wouldn't necessarily count that as a negative.

The only reason I live with my father and not my mum is because my father has a very well-paid job, money in the bank and a comfortable home in a very good area close to my school, which is supposed to be one of the best (talk about a contradiction in terms). In short, he can provide the so called stability my mum and her unconventional, flower-power lifestyle cannot. He's agreed to pay for my clothes, pocket money and everything else he thinks I need, if she'll pay for my holiday visits to Brighton – or wherever it is she's roaming at the time. But Mum's got zero money savvy and this is only my fourth visit since their divorce one year and one month ago (although she was in India on a sponsored spiritual retreat for two months of that time, so I couldn't have visited her anyway).

'No, I'm not really feeling left out,' I finally answer. You've got to feel left in before you can feel left out. My talking thoughts can be insightful. 'They're just irritating, that's all. And it's no fun without you around.' Mum may not have a white picket fence, a black bank balance or buns of steel, but she's got enough laughter stockpiled in her belly to light up London.

'I don't expect your father and Shifty feel quite the same way,' Mum chuckles as she pulls into the driveway of the tiny, lopsided beach cottage she shares with one of her New Age cronies called Lotus. She used her divorce settlement to pay for her half of the place, which means my father actually has two uses (I'm supposedly the other one).

Mum springs from the car and strides toward the front door with the sign that reads: With the Power of Love Comes Peace in the World. I can't actually see the words – I'm still staring out and gulping down the wind, but I have them memorised by heart.

It's now too black for me to actually see the ocean, but I can hear her pounding her fists against the rocks and taste her agitated salty breath on my face. I feel her force against me and imagine her tossing her dark curls with their foamy highlights into the air. She's a diva who doesn't like the night that hides her fierce beauty, but she'll be calmer by dawn. No matter how moody and unpredictable she is, if it were up to me I'd never leave her side. There's a lot to be said for living beside something so beautiful and powerful it only answers to the moon.

'Come along,' Mum calls out excitedly while her kaftan flicks and cracks in the breeze. I turn my back on the ocean.

Not much has changed since my last visit and the interior of the cottage is still warm and glowing with soft lighting and creamy neutral colours. There's a brown hessian rug spread across the wooden floor, a long, low-slung table made out of railway sleepers, and instead of a sofa, the table is fringed with oversized floor cushions covered with embroidery and patchworks of shiny material. You won't find a television anywhere either and the lounge is where most of their om'ing and meditating takes place.

Beyond this room is the small dining area, which has an old blocked fireplace and a round table with upright chairs. The surface of the table is usually camouflaged by open books, strewn papers and more unusual things like vials of patchouli oil and glinting crystal prisms. Still, Mum does try and tidy it up when I visit. There's also a single futon couch so this doubles up as my bedroom, but I don't really mind the clutter. It makes a change from the buffed, shiny surfaces I'm usually surrounded by. Mum did offer to let me share her double bed (she thought it would be fun – like a 'slumber party'), but I'm definitely too old to sleep with my mum.

'Lotus said to tell you *abhivandana*,' Mum grins and bows her head in welcome.

That's guru talk; I don't even ask any more.

'And she's very sorry she couldn't be here, although she has left us something special for our supper.'

'I can't wait,' I mumble and concentrate on shoving my backpack in the corner of the dining room beside the futon. Unless you're into soya, beet fibre, tofu or rice milk, none of the food Mum, Lotus or any of her friends rustle up is worth getting your taste buds in a spin over. 'So where is Lotus?' I ask. That's the cool thing about my mum's mates – I don't have to call them Mrs What's-it or Aunty Thingamajig. We're on a first name basis. Mum said I should start calling her by her first name too, but I think this was just another ploy to drive my father loco. And it worked. I didn't call her Iris for very long.

'Lotus is preparing for the Renaissance Fair tomorrow,' Mum replies. 'I did tell you about the Renaissance Fair, didn't I?'

'Nope,' I sigh, already expecting the worst.

'Well it's a psychic, health and visionary art fair and it's being held at the Santa Nova showground,' Mum explains. 'And along with the usual booths and fabulous stalls, this year we're featuring well-known speakers and performers of world music, as well as an exhibition of metaphysical and fantasy paintings and graphics by some of the finest New Age artists around. It'll be the biggest Renaissance Fair yet!'

So much for our mother-daughter bonding weekend then. 'Woohoo,' I grumble softly. It sounds about as appealing as taking a Lamaze child birthing class with Misty. Mum has moved to the kitchen and is too busy clattering about to notice my lack of enthusiasm. So what's new? She finally emerges carrying a bamboo tray laid with two plates, a carton of chilled rice drink and a couple of glasses, which she sets down on the dining-room table.

'Grubs up,' she sings. I peek fearfully at the dinner plates and happily discover that we're having tortillas packed with cheese, sour cream and avocado for our supper. So they're wholewheat tortillas, but at least this is real food.

'I told you Lotus was making you something special!' Mum says, spying my delight.

'I always did like Lotus,' I smile in return and slither into a chair.

We spend the next few minutes chewing silently on our nutty tortillas. I'm thinking about the pants Renaissance Fair and how it's just typically bad timing, which is the story of my life. I don't know what's keeping Mum's thoughts busy but I'm about to find out. She takes a long sip of her non-dairy, organic rice drink and finally forces her way through the silent space pushing between us. 'So what's up Lib?'

'What do you mean?' I ask through mouthfuls of avocado-green tortilla bits.

'Well, as much as I'm happy to see you darling, you are spending your school holidays with me. And that's only three weeks away. So how come you insisted on travelling all this way just for a weekend? It's not the money; I'm just concerned. Is everything OK?'

My mum really doesn't get it. How do I even begin to explain to her that being separated from her is making me sick? Worse still, how do I tell her that I might not even be around in three weeks' time? I could quite possibly be singing with the angels by then. I had to come; this may be the last time we have together.

'Tomorrow's your birthday, what were you expecting?' I finally answer, opting for the much simpler explanation instead. I even manage to look her in the eye.

'My birthday?' she caws dramatically and throws her head back. 'You know I don't acknowledge or even believe in birthdays. I'm the age of my soul not my body, darling. And my soul is centuries old – way too old for birthdays.'

Sigh, if I had a pebble for every time I'd heard that one I'd have my own private beach by now. 'Birthdays are good for you,' I reply. 'The more you have the longer you live.' You can't argue with airtight logic.

'This is also good for you,' Mum counters, holding up her glass, sloshing with the cloudy rice drink that tastes like potting soil. 'Now drink up, we have an early start in the morning.'

three
the sea, my mum and me

We've woken up to one of those fresh spring mornings that make you want to wave to strangers and kick your heels up. And I would be jolly, if I didn't have a moronic New Age Renaissance Fair to go to. It's still early and so far the car park of the Santa Nova showground is only open to the organisers and stall holders. Mum has her pick of spaces, which is just as well because she parks with her ears. Poor battered Aurora has the scars to prove it.

Mum switches the engine off and pushes the driver's door open using her foot, but doesn't get out. With hands on her hips, she pulls deeply at the fresh morning air, grinning happily. I'm not usually a fan-club president of my mum's dress sense, but I have to admit that today she looks striking. Her hair is even whiter in the sunlight and sparkling with small crystal flower hairclips. She's dressed in an indigo diamond-stitched skirt, a white embroidered top with wide sleeves, a pair of soft leather sandals, and she has her Moonstone faith cross around her neck. I stare at the pretty pink flowers she's painted on her toenails and suddenly feel horribly faded sitting next to my dear mum who always stares out at the world with bright eyes, like it's just out of the box and breathtaking.

'Hey sleepy, you coming?' She jabs me gently in my side with her fingertip.

'Uh sure,' I mumble, hooking the string of my cotton purse around my neck and grabbing my library copy of *Reincarnation for Believers* along with the black notebook I call my doodlebook. I make notes and draw diagrams of things. It's just something I do. We set out across the car park together, Mum with her woven basket decorated with knotted scarves and me staring at the ground, searching for stones to kick.

'Now I'm going to be all over the place today, Libby,' she explains, speed-walking toward the organisers' tent. So what's new, my talking thoughts bleat. 'I've got to make sure everything runs smoothly, so you can either hang out with me or go exploring, or both. We'll make the organisers' tent our HQ, all right? That way if we lose each other we'll know where to find one other again.' If only our lives were really that simple. 'Are you happy with that?' Mum asks, blinking at me nervously. Yes, you should feel guilty for leaving me, I judge her.

'Sure,' I shrug. I don't want to ruin the day.

'Fab,' she grins broadly and stops to emergency-land a big wet kiss on my lips before I can turn my head away. I really wish she wouldn't do that in public.

'Oi, IRIS,' a man's voice shouts loudly from the direction of the organisers' tent. 'Hello there lovely lady!' He blows Mum a kiss and seals the deal with a big cheesy wink. I wonder if he's that friendly to everyone.

Mum wiggles her fingers merrily at the tall man with shoulder-length silvery-blonde hair wearing a cowboy hat and cut-off denims that are way too short and tight for somebody hurtling towards middle age. His legs are tanned dark and I can't help noticing that he has very skinny calves. The man has legs like chicken drumsticks.

'I've got to get busy,' Mum declares breathlessly and shoves a tenner in my pocket. 'Now are you OK?'

'Yes, I'm fine. I'll see you later.' You rush off to Mr Kentucky Fried Chicken. I set off walking before she can do the mashed-potato-lips thing again.

The fair's various stalls and booths have been laid out in a wide circle around a stage area in the middle of the field, which must be where the speakers and New Age musos are going to be strutting their stuff and selling crazy. Most of the stalls appear to be set up and ready for business so I decide to start at one end and hope to work my way around before the tie-dyed masses show up. I'd give anything for a can of fizzy right now. Mum's homemade ginger-apricot tea tastes just like window cleaner smells and my mouth hasn't forgotten. I survey my surroundings. It's unlikely that I'll find sugary soft drinks with ingredients abbreviated to chemical symbols anywhere here today. Plenty of rice drink though, I'm sure. *Sigh.* If I keep on sighing I'm going to deflate.

The first stall is a small green and white striped marquee with a chalkboard on an easel at the entrance that says 'Healing Flower Essences' in differently coloured letters. The large table in the centre of the tent is dressed with a careful display of delicate corked vials filled with pale liquids the colour of tea. Each vial has a neat, handwritten label, but I can't quite make out what each one says. I would step closer, but I'm worried that the beaming, burly man wearing the flare pants and brightly striped, hand-knitted jersey and standing behind the table might try and talk to me. Everyone looks very jolly today, and I have a sneaky suspicion that it's going to get irritating.

So I slowly make my way around the stalls, reading their signs but still not daring to venture too close. Tibetan Medicine, Acupuncture for Everyone, Yoga Philosophy for the Modern World, *Feng Shui* Your Life, Massage Therapy, Astrology and Your Stars, Spiritual

Storytelling…today they have it all. Other stalls sell things like natural cotton clothing, henna tattoos, tie-dyed fabrics and jewellery made out of pewter, crystal and gemstones. This fair is my father's worst nightmare come to life, my talking thoughts chuckle wickedly, which reminds me that I really should get a henna tattoo. My father expects nothing less from a weekend spent with my mum.

I hear a rumble and turn around to face the gates, which have just opened to a crowd of enthusiastic Joe Public. In the next few moments my peaceful ramble will be transformed into a game of dodgems. It's too late for the tattoo stall now. I'm no good with crowds, let alone crowds of shoppers. For some reason the lure of a good buy seems to turn intelligent, mindful people into crab-walking cretins. I spy a tall leafy tree standing solitary to the left of the gates and head in its direction, hopeful for some canopied privacy and space. Give it a few hours and the hot pink crowds will be eager for this shade, but for now they're too busy pointing and chattering. The tree and its quiet shelter are mine for the time being, except I'm not as alone as I'd hoped. Pegged into the ground, just a few metres away from me, stands a square blue tent with a small, clear, plastic window on either side. The front of the tent is open and crowned by a board painted with the words 'Earthly Delights'. Earthly delights pah. I'll bet Misty's dumb-bells that it sells things like pumpkin seeds, tarot cards and pan-flute CD compilations – and not cold cans of fizzy, cheesy crisps and *Hot Hits* CDs (*real* earthly delights!). Still, at least I have my book to take my mind off this loopy lot, I consider, smoothing out the dustcover of *Reincarnation for Believers* and wiggling deeper into the earth, willing the soft ground to take the shape of my bottom. If I'm not comfortable my mind will wander all over the place and I won't absorb a single sentence.

I start reading and just as I'm sinking into the words, something to my left starts spinning and twisting and taunting my eyeballs. I try to ignore the movement and concentrate on the page before me, but eventually curiosity beats who-gives-a-damn to the finishing post and my head snaps sideways. A boy dressed in beige cargo shorts, a red T-shirt and a tall, velvet jester hat is standing outside Earthy Delights and holding two short black rubber sticks, which he's using to twirl a slightly longer colourful rubber stick that has tassels at each end. With skilfulness and patient control, he manipulates the tasselled stick to perform lofty somersaults and flipping feats that are mesmerising. His eyes stare transfixed at the spinning stick, as if he's mentally willing it to fly and soar higher into the air. I've never seen anything like this before and I quickly forget my book and stare brazenly, secure in the knowledge that the boy is too busy with his sticks to notice my jaw trailing in the dirt.

He continues with his flipping and spinning and then with a sudden flick of his right wrist, tosses the tasselled stick high into the air. He then expertly catches it with his left hand and simultaneously turns on his heel to face me, pinning my stare down with a penetrating glare of his own. He's gone from spinning to glaring so swiftly, all I can do is snort loudly in fright. His eyebrows are puckered challengingly and I can feel his pupils boring into mine like he's drilling for oil. But he doesn't speak a word. I do my best to meet his gaze and we remain staring for what feels like a millennium, until my eyeballs turn into fireballs and I can't bear the dry burning any longer.

'Whaaaat?' I whine miserably. I've never had any talent for staring contests.

'Ha!' the brat in the hat chortles loudly. 'I win!'

'You win a punch in the chops,' I fume. 'How old are you anyway…five?' He looks about my own age actually.

'Say what you like, I still win,' he laughs and starts walking in my direction. 'They're called Chinese flower sticks. Here, have a go. It's dead easy.'

'I'd rather not; I'm trying to read my book,' I huff haughtily and drop my face down to the words in my lap. I expect the bizarre boy to either say something or remove himself, but he does neither and simply continues standing there looking at me. I try and hold out for as long as possible but quickly use up all the patience I have inside me. 'Can I help you?' I look up and bark loudly.

'You really shouldn't have been staring at me,' he replies solemnly. The corners of his eyes are crimped with mischief. 'And you know you were, so don't try and deny it.'

I torture my brain for some brilliant reply. 'I was watching the flower sticks, not *you!*' It's the best I can do on short notice.

'Glad you enjoyed the show. Maybe I should turn pro and charge.'

'And maybe I should become a supermodel and move to LA.' There, that's better, brain.

'My mum says that I shouldn't argue with girls. She says it's impossible to win. Peace?' He offers his hand and waits for me to either shake it or deliver on the punch I promised a few minutes ago. I'm staring again. I've never seen anyone with two differently coloured eyes before. The left one is black and deep; the other is a dark sapphire blue. Most of his head is taken up by the ridiculous velvet jester hat he's wearing, although some unruly strands of hair have managed to make a getaway. They're also as black as liquorice. His warm brown skin reminds me of the cinnamon buns Misty munches on when my father's not around. I'm not sure if he's striking or strange.

'Yeah, whatever,' I mumble dully and shake his hand with long, loose fingers. I'm not very good with strangers.

'The name's Sam,' he announces like he's James Bond.

'Liberty Belle,' I reply and dig my hands into the pockets of my jeans.

'That's my mum's stall over there.' Sam points to the stall called Earthly Delights.

'Uh, great.' And you're telling me this because?

'Would you like to take a look? We've got some pretty cool things in there.'

Of course I don't want to take a dumb look, but something tells me that saying yes is the quickest way to get rid of this Sam person and return to my book. 'Fine, but just for a moment,' I sigh. 'My mum will be looking for me.' Like that's likely, but it sounds plausible and it's the only excuse I can think of.

I follow him over to the blue stall and step inside.

My game plan is to be a disinterested shade of cool and hightail it out of there ASAP, but I can't block the spontaneous 'oooooh' from tunnelling through my lips. The floor of Earthly Delights is just about the only surface not covered entirely by fascinating bits and bobs in every shape and colour. There are goblets made out of recycled glass bottles, herb-scented pillows, buckets of incense sticks, crystal prisms, juggling balls, stone pocket totems, pewter fairies, glass fairies, rainsticks, Celtic crosses, windchimes…enough for forever. Each item is intricate and a carefully crafted work of art and I'm suddenly glad for the tenner growing hotter in my pocket. I turn things around in my hands and suck in the details while Sam talks to me about the fair and Brighton. He's taken the hat off and looks thankfully less of an oddball. He's quite interesting too and doesn't expect much input from my side, which suits me perfectly. I even consider hanging around for a while longer, until a cluster of eager shoppers squeeze their way in beside me and crowd the confined space. While Sam attends to a large woman with pale candyfloss hair, I slip quietly from the stall unnoticed. Sure, he's nice enough – even if he does have questionable taste in hats – but I'm in no mood for making new friends. Still, I didn't come all this way to be by myself either. I wonder if Mum takes tea breaks.

The organisers' stand is nothing more than a large rectangular canopy on poles, and I find it almost empty. Mum and the rest of the organisers are all obviously very busy organising – except for Mr Kentucky Fried Chicken, who is sprawled out on a plastic chair with his tanned feet resting on a trestle table. His cowboy hat is pulled down over his face so I'm guessing he's asleep. Or maybe he's sitting there wondering who switched the lights off.

I haven't forgotten the way he glowed at my mum. I sneak up closer and stare at his Roman sandals with the thin leather straps that tie around his brown chicken ankles. His denim hot pants are stained with flecks of paint and frayed at the hems, and he's wearing a T-shirt that says 'Vote For Pedro' on the front. Strange man; I wonder if he's Pedro. I wouldn't vote for him, unless if it were for him to move to Greasy Corner, Arkansas (and that really is a place, my talking thoughts don't make things up).

I tiptoe past him and settle at the trestle table at the other end of the tent with my black doodlebook out and open in front of me. Number two on My Dying To Do List is to write my will. This is going to take some careful thought. I turn to a fresh page and scratch the words MY LAST WILL AND TESTAMENT across the top line. I then stick my pencil in my mouth and consider where to begin. I suppose my new brother or sister will automatically get my bedroom. Come to think of it, the actual bricks and cement belong to my father, not me, so whoever claims the space after I die really is not my concern. I haven't had the room for very long anyway, so I have no sentimental attachment to it.

I picture said bedroom in my imagination and mentally work my way left to right, visualising the individual items inside the four walls my father owns. I'm staring out of unfocused eyes and using the pen to drum against my front teeth. First of all, my clothes: they may not be catwalk but my supposed best friend, Sophie, is about my size and she has a conscience, so there's a chance she'll donate whatever she doesn't want to our local *Oxfam*. Yes, she's a good choice. I write 'To Sophie Ballard I leave the entire contents of my wardrobe' next to number one in the margin, adding 'anything not wanted *must* be donated to *Oxfam*' – just in case. I've noticed some changes in her since she started fancying that Marcus boy. The next thing to consider is my collection of CDs, of which there are only eleven in total but…

'Darling!' a voice goes off in my ear like a starter's gun and shoots me a metre into the air. 'I've been looking for you, where have you been?'

Thanks Mum, if I didn't have heart problems before I definitely do now. I quickly snap my doodlebook shut and slide it onto my lap. Mr KFC aka Vote for Pedro has woken up and is gazing around blearily while mopping drool from his mouth. 'I've been around,' I mumble. I hope she didn't see my list.

'Look what I have here,' she chimes and reveals two wrapped burgers with a flourish, like she's a magician's assistant who has just performed a miraculous trick. If those are real hamburgers then maybe she has.

'Let me guess – soya patties on organic wholewheat?' I ask.

'Well…no,' Mum falters, 'they're actually multi-grain buns.'

'Ah right, well that's different then,' I smile. I know she's trying and this is the closest she can bring herself to providing me with the junk food my teenage taste buds so desperately crave.

'Let's go sit on the grass and eat these in the fresh air,' she suggests. Vote for Pedro has just noticed my mum so I quickly nod and shepherd her outdoors before he can give it any more of that 'lovely lady' business.

We sit down on the grass to munch our burgers and I actually manage to finish mine off and lick my fingers. Organic tomato sauce is the perfect camouflage for soya,

I have just discovered. Mum finishes her burger off too but doesn't seem in a hurry to be anywhere so I hand her the brown paper packet sitting patiently beside me with my books.

'Here, this is for you,' I say.

'For me? Aw! What for?' Mum gushes, even though she hasn't even opened it yet.

'Your birthday – remember?' I reply and rattle my head at the heavens. Now that Mum is into her thirties this 'age-of-my-soul-not-my-body' thing seems just a little too convenient. My talking thoughts are very observant.

'Ah right…' Mum says, looking forlorn. She hadn't forgotten, but she was trying to. She looks as if she's about to protest the concept of birthdays once again but then thinks better of it and dunks her hand into the bag instead. It re-emerges holding a windchime trailing with six delicate dolphins sculpted out of pale frosted glass. She beams and hoists it up into the breeze to listen for its tinkle, all the while cooing at the beautifully arched dolphins sparkling and shimmering in the sunlight. 'My favourite stall!' she cheers, spying the brown tag printed with the Earthly Delights logo. 'Oh darling, you really are a treasure. Thank you.'

'You're welcome.' I burn and change the subject.

'So what else do you have to do today?'

'Well, let's see. I need to hang around here for a couple more hours and then it's just you and me. I promise! And I have a little surprise for you too.'

'You do?' I sing. She's changed my train ticket from Sunday to Monday! You're absolutely right Mum; who cares what the school or my father thinks. We're independent women intent on a fabulous bonding weekend.

'The Brighton Theatre Group is putting on *Annie* – your favourite film. And I've got us two tickets to tonight's performance. So what do you think about that?'

I think that was my favourite movie when I was like four years old, but it doesn't really matter – because I wouldn't care if you bought us tickets to the moon. I really couldn't give two hoots either way. An extra day in Brighton would have made up for today, not some kiddy film. That's what I think.

four
we always want more

The blinds in the dining room don't quite close all the way and my duvet is streaked with thin slivers of moonlight that have squeezed in through the chinks. I lay there motionless, like a thief trapped by the beams of a motion detector. I mustn't move. I can feel the familiar grip of fear tightening around me, squeezing and wringing the strength from my bones. Lying in bed alone at night trapped by the inky blackness seems to do strange things to my brain. Thoughts break out of my head and begin to distort and swell into towering insecurities that leave me nervous and cringing in their shadow. Fears that seem bearable in the daylight turn ominous and overwhelming when I'm alone in the darkness. I can't explain it. They just do. I must try and focus on the birthday party Lotus just told us she has organised for tomorrow. She said it seemed like an excellent idea, especially now that I'm visiting. Yes, that's a safe thought to grab on to.

I shove past the murky thoughts jostling for space and try to find a place in my head that's quiet. Think birthday party…think birthday party…how hard can that be? It's obviously a party to celebrate the age of Mum's soul (and not the age of her body), or else she'd run a mile. Of course my train back to Manchester leaves at three, which means that Mum will have to drop me off at the station by half past two, which means I'll only be attending half the party. But Mum can race back and spend the rest of the afternoon enjoying the company of her closest friends. And once everyone's left she'll probably help Lotus clean up and then put on a CD of Gregorian chants and have one of her special silky Sunday baths lit by candles. I know her routines better than anybody, which is why I've left her a note that says, 'We're still sleeping underneath the same big sky' in the glass jar of bath salts perched on the shelf in the bathroom.

I wrote and hid all my notes to Mum earlier this evening, while she was reliving *Annie* for Lotus in the living room. This way I won't have to rush through them in the morning. I can't rush my notes to Mum. They're not just any old words scribbled on scraps of paper. Every single one means something – they're the imprints of emotions pressed from my soul. They're the things I would say if I had the power to whisper flying thoughts that could soar all the way from Manchester to

Mum's ear, and they cost me a packet in tears. I hid the note that reads, 'You may be far away, but you're in my heart to stay' in Aurora's cubby-hole, and another one saying, 'I miss having you with me' in her rolled-up yoga mat.

Crying usually makes me drowsy, but tonight sleep is just out of my reach. I'm teetering right at the edge of consciousness, but every time I feel myself toppling towards oblivion a fearful thought pushes me backwards and scratches angrily at my eyelids. When I say goodbye to Mum I usually don't know when exactly I'll be seeing her next, and my luck hasn't changed. So I have a train ticket back to Brighton booked for three weeks' time, but what good is that if there's a chance I won't even be around in three weeks' time? Of course I understand that we all have expiry dates, but it's not always easy knowing that yours is sometime soon. It's an overdose of information. That will teach me for being so in touch with my primal instincts.

This could be the last time I ever visit this small, lopsided cottage and fall asleep listening to the ocean tossing and turning – just as impatient as me for some rest. That's why I leave little notes scattered about like confetti; they may need to last Mum forever. I'll probably even miss her horrible rice drink. I try to imagine her finding the notes after I'm dead but the image sets my heart quivering so I drop it quickly.

Mum has started leaving me notes too, but she's not very good at hiding them. If I wanted to I could find them all before the train had even left Brighton station. Not that I would, it's better to save them until later.

'Wakey wakey, little matey,' a voice squawks.

I lay there with my eyes closed and try to remember. I must have fallen asleep. And it sounds like I've got myself a parrot for an alarm clock. My father is going to rupture a main artery when he finds out I've got a pet in the bedroom. I crank up an eyelid but remain horizontal while the blinds and Lotus's sunbeam smile shift into focus. I'm still at Mum's. Thank goodness.

'Hi Lotus,' I croak and feel around for my senses. It takes me almost as long to wake up as it does for me to fall asleep.

'I brought you some delicious ginger-apricot tea, love,' Lotus smiles gently, revealing the familiar gap between her front teeth. She's still dressed in her long cotton nightie and her wispy hair is tangled up like tumbleweed.

I breathe deeply and then wish I hadn't. 'Is that what it is? I thought you were doing the windows,' I chuckle hoarsely, cracking a joke at the expense of Mum's pongy tea. For somebody who doesn't like mornings, today I'm stand-up hilarious.

'It's gone ten-thirty you know,' Lotus clucks and busies herself with the blinds.

'What?' I shout, shielding my prickly morning eyes from the glare of the sunlight that's suddenly saturated the dining room. Today is my last day! 'Why did you let me sleep?'

Lotus is about to protest when Mum makes an appearance. She swoops down to land a kiss on my forehead. 'Morning darling. Sleep well? Good.' She rubs my head and squeezes my cheek. 'Now go get yourself dressed and come join me in the kitchen. We're making snacks for the party and I'm busy with your favourite sandwich filling: hummus and roasted vegetable.'

I actually slept terribly, thanks. And as for my favourite filling – just because a bite of hummus and vegetable sandwich once made a one-way trip down my gullet doesn't quite make it my all-time favourite snack. My talking thoughts are in a mood this morning. Half-past ten! What were they thinking?

I plod along the corridor to the bathroom and lock myself inside. But I don't begin washing or brushing and simply stare at my reflection while my forehead props up the mirror instead. Life is too complicated in the morning. I have hair like dried grass. I've been trying to grow the stuff since I was like three but when it's not sticking out all over the place it still only touches my shoulders. It's thick and wavy and a yellow-brown colour Mum calls fawn. My friend Sophie's brother has a fawn pet rat.

The rest of my face is just your basic model equipped with very standard features: two greeny-brown eyes; one nose – average size with a bit of a dip at the end; a full set of teeth that may need braces 'but that's what all orthodontists say' (a quote from the father figure); and skin that has an oily T-bar, which is definitely standard if you're locking horns with puberty. I didn't come with any added extras like high cheekbones or pouty lips. As for my bodywork, I'm a bit of a straight-up-and-downer. I'm not fat but I'm not skinny either, and I'm still waiting for some boobage (although I don't think I'm going to suit boobs anyway so what's the difference). I'm a reliable but bottom-of-the-range economy model of a human being.

'Poor old Liberty Belle,' I groan out loud and mist up the mirror with my morning breath. So let's brush before we try that again. I peel my image from the mirror and focus on improving my a.m. appearance with the help of soap, water and various brushes, and emerge from the bathroom a short while later, scrubbed up and ready to face the day with hygiene on my side at least. And if the pot-clanging and cupboard-banging is anything to go by, Mum and Lotus are still very busy in the kitchen. I should have stayed in the bathroom.

'Ah Libby!' Mum exclaims when she spots me standing at the kitchen door. 'Look what Lotus made for me.'

You mean while you let me sleep? My talking thoughts are at it today. I amble over and take a casual peek at what's got Mum so revved up. It's a cake. And it's bright yellow. 'What's that funny eight-shaped thing in icing on the top?' I ask, trying not to sound sulky but not really succeeding.

'Isn't it brilliant?' Mum gushes. 'It's a protection symbol that represents infinity.'

'Uh, right…' I mutter. It looks like the mask of Zorro. 'Happy Birthday Iris's Soul' wouldn't have done it then?

'It means that my soul will go on forever – into infinity,' Mum continues. Sounds tiring. 'And it's a gluten-free lemon cake…' her voice trails off. I've obviously hurt her feelings. So what's new, I'm always the one left holding the guilt.

'Well, you guys certainly have been busy,' I observe

while cheerily rubbing my palms together. Every kitchen countertop is heavy with manicured snacks that promise to make us radiant, regular and mucus-free. 'So what exactly are we having then?'

'We've got fruit chips made out of air-dried slices of apple and mango, there's rice crackers with spinach and artichoke-heart dip, sultana fruit slices, salt-free trail mix, sprouted-wheat breadsticks, trays of finger sandwiches and bowls of fruit and unsalted nuts.' Mum's selling the food like she's head chef at an all-you-can-eat buffet.

I think there'll probably be enough nuts here today, my thoughts muse. 'Cool,' I say instead and grin like it's my birthday too.

'Would you mind helping me set up the Zen room for our simultaneous meditation and prayer session?' Lotus asks me. Calling it the living room would just be too normal.

'Sure,' I nod and simply follow her lead. I don't even want to know.

By the time the house is ready and the food is laid out it's almost time for the guests to arrive and I'm suddenly aware that I only have two hours and forty-six minutes left with my mum. The realisation karate chops me in the windpipe and, in a flurry of panic, I call out her name and scuttle to find her.

'Here I am,' she suddenly appears, panting at the front door. 'I was just putting out the rubbish. What's the matter? Is everything OK?'

'Uh yeh, 'course,' I mutter, standing still and trying to sound flippant. So that was very uncool, but I have other things to worry about right now. I need to spend the next two hours and forty-six minutes at my mum's side. Make that forty-five minutes.

'Droonkher tashi delek, Iris!' a voice suddenly booms from somewhere behind Mum, who spins around and nearly blacks out in fright.

'Oh, Mick,' she gasps. 'You scared me. Please – come inside.'

Mick is Mr KFC aka Vote for Pedro, and the only smidgen of good news is that instead of the denim hot pants, today his brown drumsticks are dressed in respectable full-length jeans.

'That was Tibetan for "Happy birthday Iris",' Chicken Mick chortles like he just memorised the whole entire Tibetan language instead of three measly words. He's clutching a parcel wrapped in lilac paper decorated with a tiny bunch of dried lavender. 'Here, this is for you,' he offers Mum, adding a hug and a very long kiss on her cheek to complete the package presentation. My talking thoughts counted four seconds, which sounds short but isn't for a kiss. Sicko. The signs were all there from the start.

'You are a sweetheart,' Mum coos and transports the gift to the table. 'Although you do know I'm the age of my soul, not my body.' Yeah right. She waves me over excitedly and I don't have the heart to refuse. 'Mick, this is my daughter, Libby.'

'The name's Liberty.' I swagger like I just stepped out of a trashy detective novel.

'Hi, and I'm Mick,' he replies.

Yeah whatever, Chicken Mick, I glare at him so that he knows I know he's got the hots for my mum. The doorbell chimes and Mum swallows nervously. 'Help yourself to some snacks,' she offers a little too loudly and heads for the door. I think she meant Mick, but I have to do something so I scoot over to the snacks and shove an entire finger sandwich in my mouth. Ugh! It's crunchy and disgusting; it might as well be a real finger sandwich. I need a serviette.

'Gloria,' Mum exclaims happily, 'and Sam; how lovely to see you both.' *Sam?* I nearly choke on the finger. Still, I suppose it's a fairly common name. I glance around at the door. There are no accidents; only plans other people don't tell you about. Of course Sam doesn't appear surprised to see me one bit and he marches confidently over to where I'm standing.

'Well hello Libby,' he grins. The blue eye is so dark it's almost indigo.

'Uh, mmm.' I still have finger sandwich in my mouth. I brace myself and swallow. My eyeballs are watering.

'Are you OK?'

Gulp. 'Fine.'

'Here, I brought you this,' he says, offering me a long, thin parcel wrapped up in creased brown paper that looks recycled.

I don't move. 'It's my mum's birthday, not mine.'

'I know that,' he smiles smugly. 'Gloria has your mum's gift. But I thought you might like this.'

I still don't move. 'Who is Gloria?'

'She's my mum,' he replies, extending the brown paper parcel even further. He must look like his father, because Gloria is very small and pale and blonde – everything Sam is not. I still don't budge a muscle.

'How do you know my mum?'

'Gloria is mates with Iris! Now do you want this or not?' He rattles the gift impatiently.

'I guess so,' I shrug and reach for it. The paper falls away easily and I find myself holding a set of those rubber stick things. 'Uh, what are they called again?'

'Chinese flower sticks.'

'Ah right. Well thanks for the flower sticks,' I say and smile for the first time. 'It might take me a while to get the hang of these things though.'

'That was my very first set of flower sticks. They taught me everything I know and they'll do the same for you too. I could show you some tricks, if you like,' he offers.

How do I tell him that I only have…um, about two hours and twenty-something minutes left with my mum and zero time for flower sticks? I've been watching Mum welcome the stop-start stream of hippy guests at the front door; she's glowing. Maybe living in suburbia with my father and me really was hell for her. I'm happy she's happy, except she's so busy making up for all that lost time she doesn't seem to realise that I'm falling way behind.

Before I can reject Sam's offer Lotus claps her hands and coughs loudly for effect. 'Can I have everyone's attention please,' she begins. 'We're about to start our simultaneous meditation and prayer session—' But before she can squeeze another syllable out everyone suddenly clambers towards the living-slash-Zen room and settles into a space on the floor, draping their limp, upturned wrists over their criss-crossed legs. These New Agers are an eager lot.

Just then Mum appears beside me looking shiny and excited. 'Are you going to join us?' she asks.

'What exactly would I be joining?' I can't keep the suspicion from my voice.

'By meditating and praying together we're sharing a moment of unified global consciousness and using love, compassion and understanding to heal the social, ecological and spiritual challenges before us. We're focusing our attention on our interconnected relationship with Gaia.'

Right. I did ask. 'Who is Gaia?' There I go again.

'Gaia is the living earth, named after the Greek Earth Goddess.' Mum smiles serenely.

'Course it is, I smile back. *Ker-azy*. 'I think I'll sit this one out, thanks Mum.'

'And I'll hang out with Libby, thanks Iris,' Sam pipes up.

Mum nods and quickly scuttles over to find her place amongst the group who have already begun rocking and oh'ming like they're hoping to levitate into the third dimension any second now.

'Are you ready for your first lesson in flower sticks then?' Sam whispers. I don't really want to leave Mum but it seems I've already lost her to the living earth so what's the point in hanging about and watching. I nod my head and follow him outside.

'It's really easy. Right, now copy me,' he instructs, standing square with his knees slightly bent. 'What you want to concentrate on first is getting a feel for the tasselled stick as it's supported and controlled by your shorter hand sticks. Just bounce it about like this for a while,' he says, bouncing an imaginary set of flower sticks in his hands.

To be honest, I'd rather down a bucket of rice drink. I have way too much to worry about to put my mind to bouncing rubber sticks. The only way I can resist the urge to hurry back inside is to remind myself that Mum is in a conference call with Gaia and I really have nowhere else to be. The dismal reality of the situation leads me to follow Sam's suggestion. I suppose it'll take my mind off my misery. That's something.

'So Gloria says you're going back to your dad in Manchester today,' he launches the small talk.

Bounce. Bounce. 'And she'd be right,' I reply tersely. Bounce. Bounce. A hard ball of emotion has rolled up my windpipe and lodged itself at the back of my throat. I swallow hard, forcing it back down again. The day is slipping away and I'm playing with daft rubber sticks while my mum is bonding with the planet. I think I'm about to have a panic attack.

'She said you were coming back again soon though,' he adds anxiously. 'That'll be cool, huh?'

Bounce. Bounce. 'And what would you know about it!' I blurt out and let the tasselled stick drop to the ground. I didn't mean to snap; but right now I'm a live wire dangling perilously in the breeze.

'Er, not much, I guess...' he replies and quickly changes the subject. 'Don't give up on your flower sticks. It took me months to find my rhythm – I had two left hands! Once I got so angry with them I natter natter...all the way down the blabbety blab...and swore I'd never and so on and so on.'

I'm not listening to Sam, but I'm grateful that he's filling the space with noise and trying to make today seem as normal as possible. We remain outside talking about who knows what for who knows how long; he takes care of the conversation while I toss the odd comment in here and there, stoking his chatter to keep it from growing silent and cold. Finally Mum appears at the door, looking slightly anxious. A bit late for that now, my talking thoughts brood.

The train back to Manchester is almost empty and if nobody decides to swap seats or play musical carriages, I should be able to make it through the journey without having to fend off sticky weirdo eyeballs. Saying goodbye to Mum is bad enough without having to do it in public. If the pitying half-smiles and fleeting nervous looks are anything to go by you'd easily think I was the first person to ever blub at a train station. They're only sad, old, salty tears, not nuclear acid.

Mum was a little confused by my sobs. 'I'm seeing you in three weeks' time,' she kept repeating over and over like one of her meditation mantras. But then Mum doesn't know about the dying thing, does she? Anything can happen in three weeks – and is likely to happen too. Mum doesn't know what I know, or sense the things I do. And even if I did tell her she wouldn't believe me anyway. Once again I'm left to figure everything out and face the fear on my own. You'd think I'd be used to it by now, that I'd have accepted that my parents are too busy polishing their shiny new lives to notice that something is wrong. Don't they realise that it's because of them that I don't fit in anywhere…that I don't belong any more? Three weeks shmeeks!

My black book is open and I'm trying to keep my head down and finish my Last Will and Testament, but it's not a good angle for me right now and my eyes keep welling up and my nose won't stop drip-dripping. Everything about me has changed since I started dreaming about dying and realised what it meant. But my parents haven't even glanced up. The thought of never seeing Mum again sucks my breath up and reverses it down my throat like a fireball caught in a back draught, leaving my chest burning and breathless. It just hurts so much. My top lip is blistered with sweat and the tears slipping down my cheeks are as hot and thick as blood. I think my eyes are bleeding.

Mum and I hardly spoke during the drive to the station. We just stared ahead at the road and touched fingers. On the platform waiting to board the train we made watery eye contact and gave each other a thousand quivering hugs, but we didn't really speak. And yet I still have so much to say. These visits are unnatural. We only have a certain number of hours together and we're forced to cram all the love and life we have inside us into that allotted time, whether we're up for it or not. It's contrived and not the right sort of relationship for a mum and a daughter. Being apart is a waste of precious time.

I turn the soggy page of my book and attempt to see through the mist to the words in front of me. My father will no doubt keep my computer – regardless of who I leave it to, so I might as well give it to him in the first place. It was a birthday gift, but it came with a set of conditions. I had to pass Year Eight with top marks, commit to washing his car every Saturday and agree to do the dinner dishes every night. Of course a verbal promise was not enough and in true Mackenzie Belle (that's my father's name – not a lawyer's firm, although they have so much in common) style I had to sign a promissory note. My father is as rigid as a cane, and about as much fun. Next to number three on my will I write: to my father I leave my computer.

The gentle pulsing of the train is pushing me deeper and deeper towards the dim depths of sleep. My eyelids are slipping, my chin is dipping towards my chest and before I can make one final grab at consciousness I'm officially closed for business. But my sleep is dreamless and unbroken and when I eventually come to, I have a patch of warm drool on my shirt and a view of Manchester train station out of the window. My father is standing on the platform with his arms crossed and his shoulders hunched while he balefully tracks the slowing train. My watch says that it's gone eight o'clock; he's missing news hour and his evening cup of tea, which makes me as popular as fluorescent lighting at a disco. I heave my backpack over my shoulder and lurch towards the doors, ready to spring the instant they open.

He spies me approaching and begins striding in my direction with his sinewy arms still locked, which is not a good sign. His bushy, salt-and-pepper hair is uncharacteristically ruffled and his puckered eyebrows are an irritated V-shape. 'I have been standing here for twenty minutes,' he greets me.

'Hi Dad,' I murmur. Nice to see you too, my talking thoughts add dryly.

'Really Liberty,' he begins the lecture, 'you have school in the morning and I have work. You're seeing Your Mother soon enough, this is all really quite unnecessary.' I don't say anything and lumber along beside him, rolling with the weight of my backpack. 'Misty is giving birth in just a few weeks, you know that. I really shouldn't be leaving her alone like this.' Misty pregnant? Really? That's only the seven zillionth time I've heard about it, you really should mention it more. 'And I'm not feeling particularly well,' he continues, 'heaven alone only knows what coming out at this time of night is going to do for my chest cold.' Yes, you might lose your voice. And I very much doubt heaven wants to get involved. It's just as well my talking thoughts stay in my head; I might find myself in deep trouble otherwise.

We drive the fifteen minutes home in silence. He doesn't ask about my weekend and I don't ask about his. I'd rather stab a flower stick in my eye. When we eventually walk through the front door Misty is beached on the couch and watching the instructional video for her *StairMaster*. She sees my father and her face instantly scrunches up into a pout.

'I couldn't reach my tea and now its gone cold,' she whimpers. She may be ripe and ready to burst but she's still managed to squeeze into her beloved pink velour tracksuit, which is now straining at the seams, I notice. She has the longest hair of anyone I know and the fuzzy blonde ends are fanned out across her pregnant watermelon front and snagging on everything as usual. Misty doesn't do haircuts because like Samson, she believes her hair is her strength. Her favourite things in the whole entire world are her vast collection of hair accessories, her St Tropez fake tan and the VIP gym membership card dangling from her keychain.

'Sorry petal,' my father grunts and scoops the teacup

into his hand. 'The train was late,' he mutters and strides towards the kitchen. Misty stares blankly up at me for a few moments, as if trying to place me. Sometimes I can't help wondering if her dumb act is not just her way of avoiding me as much as possible.

'Hiya Misty,' I say and head for the stairs. I don't hear her reply, but that's probably because she's still trying to remember my name.

The upstairs landing is cluttered with a workout mat and Misty's set of pink dumb-bells. She must be the only eight-and-something-month pregnant woman who still lifts weights and now that the third bedroom has been transformed into a nursery, she's forced to do this working out on the landing. I've heard them muttering that this house isn't big enough; I just filled in the blanks. My father approaches parenthood with a sense of duty. He feels a little sorry for me because I have half my mum's crazy genes, and he figures the least he can do is raise me according to the Mackenzie Belle technique and hope and pray that I don't turn out to be a lunatic serial killer who will bring shame to his good family name. That's his way of thinking, anyway. I've heard him explaining it to Misty half a dozen times and he always says it like he's saving the world. I don't know why he bothers; I don't feel like a Belle anyway. Mum chose the name Liberty at least; she insisted that since I got his surname, my first name would be her choice.

I had left my bedroom door closed but I'm not in the least bit surprised to find it wide open. I'm always being told to stop hiding behind closed doors. My father believes that he's rescuing me from myself. He also says that only once I've earned his trust and respect will I be shown trust and respect, but what he doesn't realise is that all he's doing is fuelling the flames of rebellion. And he's made earning his respect about as attractive as growing chest hair.

I close the bedroom door behind me and heave my backpack onto the bedcover embroidered with moons and stars that Mum bought me. The quicker I go to sleep the less interaction I need to have with Commando Ken and Workout Barbie. I quickly unzip my backpack, turn it upside down and keep on shaking until its insides are strewn out across the bed. I then sort my clothes into two piles – clean clothes and those that aren't. That's when I notice a small square of folded paper sticking out of my toiletry bag. It smells of Mum's musky perfume. It's definitely a note. I unfold it with unsteady fingers.

'Neither time nor distance could ever separate us,' I read softly. Two threads of fresh tears start rolling down the salty track left by the tears that dried on the train. Sadness stretches my mouth ugly and my cheeks tighten and press up against my eyes – squeezing more tears from my ducts. I miss her so much already. Just then my bedroom door tap-taps and swings open, revealing my father in all his blue-check pyjama'd glory. That wasn't a knock but rather his way of announcing his arrival.

'Can't you ever knock?' I sob in frustration.

He stops and stares at me with eyebrows that are sitting high up on his forehead. He's surprised by my eruption and is trying to work out what just happened to upset me. Suddenly his eyes widen in recognition. 'We're not starting *that* again, are we?' he mutters with just a hint of pleading in his voice. He's not completely heartless. 'Liberty, must we put up with these episodes *every* time you visit Your Mother? It's not fair on the rest of us. You really must try and focus on others instead of yourself for a while,' he sermons.

'Oh Dad, just forget it,' I sniff, swallow and dry my eyes on my fists. I suppose I shouldn't feel angry – he tells *everyone* what they should and shouldn't be doing. I turn my back on him, tuck Mum's note in my pocket and continue sorting through my backpack.

'It's really not *our* fault Your Mother moved to Brighton,' he adds softly, balancing his hand uncomfortably on my shoulder. That's my father's touchy-feely side then. And why must everything include Shifty! One of these days my talking thoughts are going to bounce right out of my head. 'I think we all need to remember that there's a baby on the way and a certain mother-to-be needs all the support she can get,' he continues. 'You should be giving instead of taking, Liberty. It's not always about you, you'll learn that when you're older. Now,' he concludes, tapping me softly on the shoulder with the flat of his palm like he's at the petting zoo, 'do you think you can buck yourself up? Change gears on that attitude, huh?' My father is a travel agent for guilt trips.

I keep my back to him and close my eyes to count to ten and pray for strength and sanity. Nobody can ever understand what it's like to have your mum for your entire life and then to one day suddenly not have her around any more. In some ways divorce is worse than death. There are many ways to lose someone you love. It doesn't hurt any less.

six
teenage kicks

My first lesson of the day is double maths, which is also my worst lesson of the day. For some reason I have a mental block against all numbers above ten. I think it may have something to do with the fact that I only have as many fingers and I need them all to count with. I'm stuck once I'm out of fingers. The one thing I am rather good at is my times table, but that's only because I've got a good memory for repetitive sounds. Play me a song once and I can just about sing it back word for word. It would be a gift, if I didn't have a voice like a test signal. Rather like my talking thoughts, the universe has a dark sense of humour.

My friend Sophie sits directly behind me and I find her at her desk chatting away to Evie, who is also our friend and sits at the desk alongside Sophie's.

'Hey!' I grin big enough for two.

'Oh hiya,' Sophie sings breezily but doesn't meet my eye. In fact, she's barely glanced up at me; this doesn't look good. 'So we chatted for a bit and he kissed me – lips no tongue – and said he'd definitely call,' she says to Evie. Her spine is rigid and she's posing coyly with her hands clasping her knees while her face is animated and beaming like she's doing a live interview. 'I can't remember a single thing about the movie though! Ha ha ha.' Evie also thinks this is very funny.

'What movie?' I ask as I take my seat.

'Oh, just some movie.' Sophie grins and winks at Evie.

Right. Let me guess. Could a daft date with that Marcus person have something to do with this conversation? Both girls are silent and slip each other knowing little peeks while I look on and wonder what crucial nugget of information I've missed out on. It's very important to be up to speed with the latest gossip. To be uninformed is social suicide because everybody will assume that you're out of the loop and also stop telling you things. Once set in motion, it's a vicious circle that quickly creates outcasts of once good-enough teenagers.

Sophie is supposed to be my best friend but she goes off me every so often. Her dad died when she was young and she now lives with her mum, sister and brother. Her mum remarried but her second husband – Sophie's stepfather – is the captain of a cargo ship and usually away at sea. He brings the money home and disappears again. He's nice enough, but detached in a way that you don't really notice whether he's there or not. Sophie's mum also needs to take regular breaks from raising three kids and so she's converted the garage attached to their house into her own private sanctuary, complete with a kitchenette and cosy television room. She ventures out into the rest of the house every so often to make sure that Sophie and her siblings have food and nothing has caught on fire, but for the rest of the time she keeps a safe distance. I love going to Sophie's because it's a deafening democracy – everything my home is not.

If only Evie weren't here I could tell Sophie how miserable I am and she might not do this to me now, right here, today. She might feel sorry for me and put her arms around me instead. I stare at both girls openly playing dodgems with their eyeballs like I'm blind or invisible, or both.

'OK, well that's cool,' I simply say and turn away to burrow in my bag for my algebra textbook. Sophie and I have been best friends for years and she's a good person, but she's very into being cool and having fun and I can't deny that I'm not always that much fun or very cool at all. I'm being raised in a boot camp; what chance do I have? I'm not allowed to do very much and I think Sophie gets tired of it sometimes. I suppose I can't really blame her. Being friends with me is like hanging out with a handbrake. When she's completely fed up with me she shows it by finding a new best friend for a while. But she always comes back to me, and I always take her back. I'd be a total turkey not to. I have fun with Sophie. I'm still not sure what she gets out of our friendship or what keeps her coming back to me. Maybe she feels comfortable around me? She can drop the cool act and just be herself when we're alone together. And I'm quite calm and not much of a threat. That could be it.

After maths I have computer studies and Sophie has Spanish but she doesn't seem to notice that we're headed in different directions. Or if she does she gets an Oscar for pretending she doesn't. I wish I didn't care but I do, and I spend the next lesson staring blankly at Mr Belmont pointing out the various components that make up a computer motherboard while trying unsuccessfully to catch his words as they whizz past my ears. I could self-combust – right here, right now – and take the wooden chair with me, and I don't think anybody would even look up. I can just picture it – after I die, it'll be all everybody talks about. But they'll be saying, 'No way! Oh, Liberty Belle. So which one was she again?' If Sophie or Evie died they'd have a collective embolism and blither on about how much the girls had to live for, boo hoo. My self-pity is as wide and deep as the Grand Canyon.

The bell sounds and my talking thoughts wonder if break times are really that necessary. If we cut them out completely we could be home a whole hour earlier at least, which isn't altogether that tantalising but right now it's the bluntest knife I'm holding. A part of my brain considers skipping lunch and my friends altogether but I don't want to make things any worse with Sophie and who knows, I could be imagining it all. I've been called oversensitive once or twice before. Maybe she really wants to hear about my weekend with Mum. So I push myself down to the quad and find my four closest friends sitting in a circle against the wall where we always sit. Sophie is recounting the kiss-on-the-lips-but-no-tongue story and everyone is superglued to her words, like she just lost her virginity or something. There's a narrow space between Evie and our friend Jasmine so I aim for it and hope they'll shift over. They don't, but I sit down anyway – just slightly outside of the group, and listen with an expression like I've heard the story before but it's definitely still interesting enough to listen to again. Being a teen is like taking part in a reality television show – it's all about teams, schemes and taking it one step at a time.

Sophie eventually loses the stage to Jasmine, whose older brother had a 'wicked' house party she was allowed to stick around for. Our other friend Keisha went with her family to Butlins and had 'like the best time ever'. As I sit there listening to my friends each trying to outdo one other with tales of their weekend exploits, I'm suddenly very aware of how their lives contrast with my own. Nobody asks about my weekend and I don't bother serving up any sorry details either. I know that I should participate more if I want the girls to like me – even make it up if I have to, but I just don't have the energy. Sometimes I think it's just as well I'm only making this planet a pit stop. I don't think I've got what it takes to win this reality show.

The end-of-break bell sounds and I suddenly remember that we've got compulsory try outs for our school athletics' day, and I'm down for the hurdles. I close my eyes and attempt to psyche myself up, but there's no point. I simply can't face an hour of bounding over jumps. I think racing horses over steeplechase is cruel so it really makes no sense to put myself through the same agony (and you can be sure the horses wouldn't either if they had a choice). So I split from my group of friends and slip into the library. I seem to live in my own world but that's OK, they know me here.

And a library is a good place to hide; you're not allowed to talk to anyone anyway.

I can never usually find a free computer during break times, but now that most of the kids have dawdled off to classes or are running steeplechase I have my pick. Mrs Budd, the head librarian, tracks my movements suspiciously, but if she knows I'm bunking she doesn't say anything and finally returns her attention to filing. I slide in front of the computer furthest from the library counter and open up my Hotmail. We're not allowed to use the library computers to send emails – they're meant to be used for research only, but Mrs Budd is too far away to notice and there's nobody else about, so like the rest of the world – what do I care.

My Hotmail homepage says that I have five new messages. I suck in my breath and hope that somewhere amongst the *you're-a-prize-winner* junk mails is a mail from Mum. I click on the Inbox icon and wait and watch as the page slowly unfurls, and then scan the addresses for Mum's familiar iris_of_the_earth@hotmail.co.uk. Nothing. Big fat poxy surprise! As I'm ticking the boxes to delete the junk mails I notice that the second address from the bottom is thesameister@yahoo.co.uk. So it's not an uncommon name. I click-to-open anyway.

Hey Libby, Sam here. Surprised? How are the flower sticks working out? I hope you're still practising. Don't give up! Things over here in Brighton are fine. It's Sunday night and raining, which is pants. I hope it's cleared up by the weekend coz otherwise we're in for a dull old time. I don't have much planned, just school and the usual stuff. Mum took some digital photos at your Mum's (soul's :-)) birthday party. I've just downloaded them and thought you might like to see a few. See you in three weeks then!

Later,
The Sameister

PS Your mum gave me your email address by the way
PPS We should keep in touch
PPPS I hope you're not annoyed (like usual :-))

The flower sticks, I remember guiltily. They're shoved underneath my bed. The email has two attachments and I click on the first paperclip icon and impatiently wait for the file to download and open. It's a photo of Sam and me in the garden. My tongue is poking out of the corner of my mouth and my forehead is crumpled in concentration as I focus on bouncing the tasselled stick.

Sam looks like he's trying not to laugh. We look so normal and happy. That's because you can't see my eyes. Still, the afternoon would have been unbearable if it weren't for Sam and his daft flower sticks, and I can't resist the small smile tugging at the crook of my lips.

I minimise the photo and click on the second paperclip icon. This is a photo of Mum standing over her bright yellow *Mask of Zorro* birthday cake. But instead of looking at the cake she's about to cut, her head is turned and she's gazing at me with a Mona Lisa smile; she looks happy and heartbroken at the same time. I don't recall the particular moment this photo was snapped, but that's probably because I'm staring blindly at the cake and quite obviously stewing in my own thoughts. It's always this way. We waste the time we have together dreading saying goodbye. A single hot wet tear breaks loose and slides down my cheek, but I barely notice it.

'The library computers are not for checking your emails, young lady!' a voice declares. I jolt in my seat and spin around to find Mrs Budd standing behind me with her hands pinching her hips. Her eyes skip from the computer screen to my face, but neither of us speak. Something in her gaze shifts and softens ever so slightly, and after what feels like forever she finally twirls on her heel and marches back in the direction of the counter without saying another word, leaving me to it. I remain in my seat and stare at her receding figure.

seven
see you in heaven

Number five on My Dying To Do List is to make a remembrance collage for my new baby brother or sister. I've bought a large piece of white card and I plan to fill it with photos, mementoes and things that will tell my sibling a little more about me. If we never get to meet I think it's important that the kid knows that he or she once had a sister. Even if we do have some time together, it won't be much and babies don't remember anything anyway. And one day he or she might like to know that my favourite colour was orange; that I was mad about Eighties music (even if I wasn't around to experience it); that I loved Weeping Willows but was petrified of birds (even the small ones); that I really enjoyed reading and thought it was a very good idea if he or she did too; that I liked people who knew how to listen but disliked big egos; that I had a passion for the ocean and would have liked a job taking care of it one day; that my favourite treat was nougat but my worst was Turkish Delight (it tastes like air freshener); and most importantly of all – that I would have made a really good big sister and friend.

I've still got to give the collage a heading. I should probably just write 'Liberty Belle' or 'Your Big Sister' top-centre of the blank sheet of card and be done with it, but I sidestep the empty space for the moment, just in case I decide to take a more creative or dramatic route. I have a paint chip of my favourite shade of orange called Sunset, and I carefully glue it to the top right corner of the sheet of card and write the words MY FAVOURITE COLOUR below it.

One of my favourite Eighties songs is called *Sad Songs Say So Much* and it's sung by Elton John. I like the whole song, but I really like the lines, 'If someone else is suffering enough to write it down, when every single word makes sense, then it's easier to have those songs around.' I don't wish misery on anybody, but when you're feeling low it helps to know that you're not the only one in the world. I think that's a very good point and I think Elton and I are on the same wavelength.

I write the lyrics just below the Sunset paint chip and draw musical notes around it like a border. Hopefully the words will mean something to the kid one day too. I can hear Misty slowly plodding upstairs and imagine my father trailing close behind her. The sound gets closer and louder and then suddenly stops, only to be replaced by heavy breathing. She's finally made it to the landing. If she gets any bigger we're going to have to reinforce the first floor.

'Oh, I do miss you darlings,' she wails breathlessly. I think she's talking to her dumb-bells. It's a good name for them too, my talking thoughts wisecrack. At this rate the kid is going to grow up to be as deep as a puddle of mud; it's up to me to teach him or her that taking care of your mind and your soul is just as important as taking care of your body – that it's what's inside your heart that really counts. I bet the Dalai Lama has some thoughts on the subject. Just then my bedroom door tap-taps and swings open to reveal my father.

'Why must you always keep this door closed?' he groans and swipes his hand through his hair in frustration. 'We don't hide behind doors in this house, Liberty.' The way my father finds fault with everything you'd think there was some kind of reward for it.

'I was changing,' I sigh without even bothering to look up.

'I can't hear you when you're talking to the desk.'

I turn around, fold my arms across my chest and try to look as bored as I possibly can with my eyes still open. That better then? My daring disinterest is new territory for both my father and me.

'Er, what are you doing?' he snaps. He's terrified of losing control and right now he's not entirely sure who's refereeing this particular game.

'A school project,' I lie convincingly for the second time in as many minutes.

'Well, Misty and I are going to bed now,' he sniffs authoritatively. Yuck, there's information I could have done without. 'It's time for you to do the same. So lights out, OK?'

'Yeh,' I lie, third-time-lucky.

'You need to do something about your attitude!' he yaps, about-turns and marches from the room. I move to switch my desk lamp off and wait and listen for the house to dim and settle into the shadows. I eavesdrop on the silence for enough minutes to allow my eyes to adjust to the darkness before finally stealth-creeping over to the bedroom door. I close it quietly and remove my dressing gown and gently wedge it against the bottom of the door before returning to my desk to feel for the computer switch.

Like a giant eyelid snapping open, the computer screen wakes up from its sleep and instantly soaks the desk in its electric luminance. I make sure the volume on the speakers is turned all the way down and open up the Internet and begin my search for the Dalai Lama's lessons on life. I get twenty-one thousand hits. This might take a while.

I don't find one site that has all the right answers but after some patient searching and cutting and pasting I'm eventually left with a list of lessons that make a lot of sense. These should help the kid. Reading from the computer screen I begin to write each point down, one below the other, on the left-hand side of the sheet of card. I use some gold stars for decoration and call it:

How to Live Your Best Life

1. Real happiness comes from being useful.
2. Balance is a key element of a happy life. Take care to avoid extremes.
3. Inner happiness only comes about through self-esteem + self-respect + personal pride. Get these ingredients right and with careful planning the rest will fall into place.
4. Do what you love and share with others.
5. Happiness is a state of mind, so the real source of happiness must lie within your mind, not in external things. If your mind is peaceful you will be happy, regardless of your external circumstances.

6. Happiness comes from a sense of universal responsibility. We must take care of one another and the planet we share.

7. If you want others to be happy, practise compassion. If you want to be happy, practise compassion.

8. Be gentle with the earth.

9. Always give your best and you can't lose.

Number eight is for Mum – not that she deserves it. I wonder if she's found a spare second to think about me and send me an email? I dial into my Hotmail and stare mindlessly at the small digital clock flashing at the bottom-right of the screen while the page takes an aeon to load. It's 11:03 p.m. already. Make that 11:04 p.m. She might as well have posted me a letter at this rate. I've been feeling raggedy ever since my return from Brighton and I don't suppose a lack of sleep is going to help matters much. I really should go to bed this minute. I drum my fingertips on the desk and blow air up my nostrils. Ho hum. Finally the page opens. There's a mail from Mum!

My darling Libby,
How was your train trip back to Manchester? I miss

you already! Gloria's son Sam asked for your email address, so don't be surprised if you hear from him. All is well in Brighton. It's been raining since you left. Gaia is taking a nice long shower! I promise a longer mail soon.
Love and light sweetheart,
Your mum Iris x

That Gaia should take a nice long leap because she's strumming on my nerves, my talking thoughts grumble. One short mail and it's almost all about Gaia! I press the flashing button on the computer screen and finally topple into bed, sandwiching myself between the chilly cotton sheets that will take at least five minutes to warm up. But at least I got a mail from my mum.

eight
leave it to fate

My eyelids flutter open and the blackness gives way to colour. I can just make out the shape and contours of my bedroom but everything is hazy and distorted, like I'm suspended and trapped just a few centimetres below the oily surface of water. I want desperately to kick up and carve through to the outside but I'm paralysed, too heavy to move. My mind is awake but my body is still wrapped up in sleep. None of me works any more. I can't even shout. I can't do anything. I've had this happen to me before; it's called sleep paralysis. I should be less anxious. If someone could hear me then maybe they could help me. I bite down on my panic and gulp it back down my throat. If I can only guide my fear to my vocal chords then maybe I can put it to use. I lay there motionless for what feels like forever until I finally hear a burbling noise I hope is coming from somewhere inside me. If not I may just be in bigger trouble than I first thought.

The sound is a switch that suddenly trips my paralysis, instantly springing my muscles from their locks. I shoot upright – like Frankenstein's monster shocked to life – and stare out at my surroundings. I'm waiting for the room to settle and make sense once again. The sound of breathing fills up my ears. It's only 6:37 a.m.; Misty and my father must still be asleep. I lift my dressing gown from the floor, open the bedroom door and stumble through to the bathroom. The door clicks closed behind me and I yank the cord dangling from the small fluorescent tube on the wall over the sink. The shadows disappear with the speed of light and I'm surrounded by the reassuring backdrop of the peaches-and-cream bathroom that is still mine and mine alone. No stinked-out baby nappies in here yet. The face in the mirror is creased and pale. I am tired and miserable.

I move away from the mirror, drop my sleep-warm pyjama bottoms and shock my bottom with the night-chilled toilet seat. Hygiene aside, if we had a furry toilet seat cover it wouldn't take me nearly as long in the mornings. Today is strange. Everything feels different. I glance down. Everything *is* different. Everything is suddenly very very red. I stare at the brand new shock of colour leaking from me and wait for my thoughts to stop fizzing.

We know what this is, my talking thoughts reason.

Mum told us this would happen one day soon. This means I'm a woman. OK, now I'm just embarrassing myself. This is all very inconvenient. I'm not nearly ready for this yet, especially not right now. Starting your period really should be a conscious decision; too much of this puberty business is left up to the universe. It's like a haphazard game of pinball. I'm not scared and only a tiny bit fussed…I'm seriously put out though!

I rummage for the sanitary towels Mum bought me especially for this day. There they are; a travel pack of five. *Five!?* We were still a family when Mum gave these to me; I guess she forgot she wouldn't be around to buy me more. Now what? I want to phone Mum but I need privacy to do that, which does not exist in this house. I must email her before my father and his other one-and-a-half stir. I creep through to my bedroom and quickly switch on the computer screen. My Hotmail is still up so I connect to the Internet and retype my password at super speed. My father coughs. I only have a few minutes. I hastily open my Inbox, hurriedly click on Mum's email, quickly hit the reply button and immediately begin typing:

No time for chit-chat. I've just started my period and only have a stupid travel-pack of pad thingies. How long were those supposed to last me! It's just so typical that I'm left to deal with everything on my own. I hope you have a solution to this. And don't even think of telling me to go out amongst the general public and just buy more.

PS I will have a wobbler if you do, and besides I don't have any cash anyway (and I'm not asking my father because he'll want an expenditure breakdown or something).

I know my email sounds petulant and childish but I don't care. Just what am I supposed to do…casually stroll into Sainsbury's and waltz out with a gigantic bumper-pack of sanitary towels under my arm? Oh, please can I – like I'm not a social reject as it is! I wish I would just die right now. What's the point in delaying it? I am the bug on the windshield of life.

I hear my father moving around in their en-suite bathroom and hurriedly press the send button. The screen slowly disappears and is replaced by another screen with a new message:

> Your message has been sent to:
> thesameister@yahoo.co.uk

I sit and stare numbly at the screen while the information gradually drip-drips into my head and begins to settle into something that vaguely resembles the dismal truth of the situation. My brain makes a valiant attempt at damage control – desperately grappling for reasonable explanations (really, anything will do), but comes up empty, leaving me to face the cold, hard reality of what has just taken place here. My twitching fingers want to reach out and catch the email, but I know that it's already hurtling along the fast lane of the information highway, winging its way to one Sameister of Yahooville. I would scream but all I can manage is a croak. Repeatedly smash forehead on keyboard to continue, my talking thoughts advise me.

The rest of the morning is a blur. I can't think about anything else except the fact that I have just done the most embarrassing thing of my life. Sam will probably have a cracking good laugh at my expense and pass my email on to every person in the larger Brighton postal code area. I didn't even address the mail to Mum so for all I know he might think the mail was actually meant for him, in which case he's no doubt convinced that I'm off my trolley. How will I face going back there in a few weeks' time? I can't even think about that right now.

Of course if that email isn't the most embarrassing

thing ever then I suppose I've got my sanitary towel buying expedition to look forward to because as much as I'd like to block it out, I know that's what it's going to come down to. I will have committed social suicide not once – but *twice* in a single week. I wonder if I should include that on my remembrance collage, and let the kid know what a barking fool he or she had for a sister. Being good at stupid does not count. At least I'll have my straitjacket to keep me warm.

The takeaway chippie near our school has a callbox in the waiting area and when the break bell sounds I furtively scoot out of the gates before anyone can spot me and make a beeline for its door. I don't know quite what I expect Mum to do about either of my predicaments but I do expect her to do something, that much I'm sure of. She was the one who moved all the way to Brighton in the first place.

The girl with dyed red and black hair and a pincushion-face full of piercings working behind the chippie counter stalks my arrival with a suspicious frown. Oh so *she* never skived out of school! I would give her a piece of my frazzled mind but she looks like she might hurt so I head quietly over to the public phone mounted on the wall instead. The handle is opaque and greasy with chip fat but I stick it against my ear anyway and dial Mum's number. It rings fourteen times before a recorded voice finally arrives to suggest that I try again later. Right now slamming the receiver back down on its mounted cradle would bring me infinite joy, but Pinhead is scrutinising me. Her chin is lowered and her eyes are locked on me – her target – challengingly. Working here is dead boring and she's patiently waiting for any excuse to make her day more exciting. And I'm fresh meat.

I ever-so-gently replace the receiver, calmly retrieve my unused fifty pence piece from the coin slot and soundlessly shuffle out of the stagnant chippie with my eyes scraping the floor. Girls like Pinhead will merrily pop you one just for looking at them. I make it back into the school grounds and wander dismally in the direction of the extreme sport I like to call my friends, who are sitting together in the usual place with their eyes pulled wide and round. They've got their gossip goggles on again. So what's new, they're always nattering about somebody.

'Hiya,' I mutter and disintegrate on the floor between Sophie and Keisha.

'So where have you been then?' Sophie asks.

I squint at her warily, trying to decide whether her question is borne out of concern or irritation. Sophie doesn't always want to be my best friend, but she expects nothing less of me.

'I had to sort something out,' I ramble vaguely.

'We're all going to the social at the cultural centre on Saturday, aren't we?' Jasmine twitters. 'My brother says that all the blokes from the boys' school are making a turnout, so it's going to be a PAR-TY!'

We attend St John's Secondary, which has separate schools for girls and boys, although the actual buildings are only a street apart – just far enough to be out of sight but never quite far enough to be out of mind. A co-ed social is to segregated teenagers what parole is to a repeat offender.

Everyone nods excitedly and I rummage in my blazer pocket for anything. Evie is watching me carefully, deciding whether or not to push my buttons. I'm not her biggest fan – she has a mean streak. Not that it matters much; Evie likes Evie enough for everybody. She thinks she's über-cool and likes her long nails the best, making a lunchtime show of scooping the soft toffee centre of *Rolo* chocolates out with her pinkie nail and then sucking on it. It's the most yuk thing ever. When I peg it I might come back to haunt Evie. It could just about make everything worthwhile.

I don't want to be here any more and I certainly don't

want to talk about a social that I will definitely not be going to, so I hook my bag over my shoulder and quickly clamber to my feet. 'I'm not feeling well,' I sigh. 'I'm off to the sick bay for a bit.' Nobody says anything or else I'm in too much of a hurry to hear them.

The nurse on duty is sitting at a desk in the small office next to the sick bay. She's about to tackle a thick sandwich framed with bright green lettuce, which makes me an unwelcome interruption.

'I'm sick,' I announce.

'What's wrong with you?' She looks me up and down and her eyes say it all: why are you here and what can I do to change that?

'I...uh...period pains.' When in doubt, mumble. I don't really have any pains but Sophie's older sister, Kate, who is a teller at a bank says that it's an ancient excuse we're quite entitled to use. Apparently it works even better on men, but I said I couldn't imagine saying that to a bloke (apart from my email to Sam, that is). Kate shrugged and told me I'd soon change my mind.

'All right, but don't forget to take your shoes off,' the nurse growls and waves me in. 'I'm sick o' cleaning up after you lot. I'm a nurse, not a flaming maid.'

Somebody needs to work on their bedside manner, my talking thoughts rumble. I head for the farthest trolley bed, prise my shoes off and crawl under the scratchy blue government-issue blanket. I don't remember how long it takes me to nod off or how long I sleep for, but one minute I'm staring up at the pocked ceiling tiles and the next I'm staring at Sophie's head dangling over me. And she's either chewing gum or saying something.

'Libby? Lib-er-ty! Are you asleep?'

'I was.'

'Oh well,' Sophie replies, 'I must have woken you up.' So she may be prettier and more popular than me, but she's definitely not the brightest crayon in the box.

'Yes, it would seem so.' I sigh and struggle to sit up.

'So what's the matter with you then?'

'I'm just really tired,' I say. 'And I started my period this morning.'

'Ah, right then. Well, that's the way it goes, huh. It's no biggie really.'

'You don't have to go and buy your own whatchamathingies, do you?' I sniff. Sophie stares at me blankly. 'Your own sanitary towel…padthingies!' I add louder than I would have liked.

'Just ask your mum…er, step-mum to buy them for you,' is Sophie's suggestion.

'Oh please, Misty can't even fit inside a shop any more! And even if she could, we've only ever said about

96

five words to each other. Do you really think I'm in a position to casually stroll up to her and just ask her to buy me some…*you-know-whats*?'

'They're called pads, Libby. It's not a four-letter word.'

'Actually it is a four-letter word, Sophie,' I sigh, 'but I know what you mean.' I can't help it that I'm shy about this sort of thing. Sophie lives in a house where everything is discussed openly whereas I'm being raised in a very clinical environment. It's not my fault if I'm a self-conscious spazoid.

'Well, we have cupboards of the four-letter things at home; you can have a packet of mine if you like. Do you want to come to my house now?'

'Now?' I ask.

'Uh yuh, it's like home time already.'

Ah right. That means I've been sleeping for over four hours then; time flies when you're drained and miserable. I might be losing the will to live. I wouldn't necessarily have guessed it, but perhaps *that's* how I'm going to die. I can see my epitaph now: Liberty Belle – daughter, sister and friend – who lost the will to live.

nine
one step at a time

Sophie's fourteen-year-old brother Shane is at home and sprawled across the length of the living-room sofa, lovingly cradling his guitar baby. His forehead is lined and he's picking at the strings like it's brain surgery. That's how I notice that he's grown the nails of his right plucking hand. I used to have a serious love-crush on Shane, but that was before he got tall, thin and pimply. And grew his nails. He's started to smell a bit funny too.

'What have you done to your hair?' Sophie giggles. Shane's dark brown hair is now Fanta-orange.

'I used peroxide to bleach it. Babes dig blonds,' he drawls like some tempting Don Juan.

'Coooool!' Sophie laughs and waltzes through to her bedroom. Shane and Sophie consider themselves superstar fabulous – in their eyes they can do no wrong. They're almost the same age and have a lot in common, and I suppose their dad's death brought them even closer.

'It's cool by da pool. Whazz-up Libby, you dig?' Shane nods with a sly wink.

So this month we're going to be a rap star then, the thoughts chortle. 'Hey Fanta Claws,' I nod courteously and follow Sophie through to her bedroom. So that wasn't very nice, but it won't make the slightest dent in Shane's ego.

One of Sophie's favourite hobbies is rearranging her bedroom and I'm not in the least bit surprised to walk in and discover that apart from the built-in cupboard, nothing is where it used to be. I manage to find the bed and plop down on it while Sophie rummages through her chest of drawers.

'There you go,' she finally says and launches something large, square and weightless into the air. I manage to catch it with both hands. It's a bumper pack of sanitary thingies. I mean pads.

'Thanks,' I say, wondering how I'm going to carry these things home.

'I've just *got* to eat something,' Sophie sighs dramatically, deserting her bag and shoes and about-turning for the kitchen. I follow in her wake.

Sophie is tall and slim but her older sister, Kate, is short and softer and always weighing her food and consulting some diet chart she has mounted on the fridge door. And it's rubbed off on Sophie, who now counts every mouthful she eats. Everything in their kitchen is low calorie, including the general conversation. Kate is very conservative and proper, whereas Sophie is loud and social; their respective diets give them something to talk about at least.

'How about fat-free cottage cheese on Melba toast?' my friend asks me.

'Yeah sure, whatever.' I nod. No wonder Shane is so skinny, poor geezer. I probably shouldn't have called him Fanta Claws.

'So are you going to the social on Saturday then?' Sophie attempts to sound optimistic.

''Course,' I snort. 'I should get there just after hell freezes over.'

Sophie doesn't even have to ask. 'Well, if it helps, you can always sleep over here if you like.'

'He'll only want to speak to your mum first,' I sigh. 'I wish we could get Kate to pretend to be your mum. She'd definitely pull it off.'

'You know Kate, that's about as likely as your dad giving you his permission and demanding that you have a good time too.'

'I know.' I begin nibbling half-heartedly at the lunch that won't make me fat but definitely won't make me happy either. I really shouldn't be wasting my few remaining meals on this earth with low-fat anything. Who cares if you're slim and dead?

The back door opens and candid Kate appears, dressed in a cerise leotard and black sweatpants made out of baggy parachute material that chafe as she walks, making a sound like a zipper being pulled up and down, up and down. Her dark fringe is strapped to her forehead with a striped black and cerise headband that's also pulling at her eyebrows, making her look just a tiny bit surprised.

'Afternoon Liberty,' she greets me politely. Kate moves her lips just as much as she needs to in order to get the words out – not a millimetre more. Her movements are just as small and neat as she reaches for a bottle filled with low-calorie orange from the fridge. I'm about to say hello back but she's already moved on from me. 'I'm off to the gym, Sophie, are you coming with me? They're having an open day and doing all sorts of promotional things; it should be worthwhile.'

'I'm just having a snack,' Sophie replies.

'Well, all I've had today is an apricot and a granola bar,' Kate sighs, like she just spent the day collecting money for cancer research or something.

'This is the first thing I've had all day,' Sophie rallies, waving her Melba and fat-free cheese delicately in the air. 'I thought I'd better have something.'

'We could get a carrot and mango smoothie from the juice bar at the gym if you like?' Kate offers hopefully.

'Those things are soooo filling,' Sophie exhales noisily and puts her hand to her flat stomach.

'I know!' Kate caws, like *isn't that the biggest coincidence*. 'But then we'll probably need it after our workout.'

'Yes, that's true,' Sophie agrees solemnly, like between the two of them they just figured out a way to reduce third world debt. 'But it might ruin our supper.' Ah yes, there is that to consider. My talking thoughts are almost enjoying this.

'Oh, I'll probably skip supper,' Kate volleys with a slightly superior sigh.

'Well, I don't think I can even finish this!' Sophie drops her toast onto her plate, still laden with two untouched slices. 'You might as well have it, Libby.'

Uh, me? My cheeks are bulging with Melba and cheese; I knew I could get a whole one in. It'll be a while before I can talk again and both Sophie and Kate are looking at me with pity. Still, what do I care – this diet grub isn't half bad and way better than that soya stuff I eat at Mum's. I slide Sophie's plate over towards me, taking care to remove the slice she's already bitten into. I do have some standards.

'Do you want to hang about here with Shane then?' Sophie asks me.

That'll be a negative. I shake my head vehemently and raise a finger in the air to indicate that I only need a second before I can talk again. Kate has a car and Misty will be at the gym. I can get a lift home from the gym with my father when he comes to collect Misty. It'll save me and my giant packet of pads the bus trip.

'Could I get a lift to the gym with you?' I finally swallow and ask Kate.

'Yes, of course,' she smiles at me compassionately. She's always willing to help those less fortunate than herself.

'I'll just go and change then,' Sophie announces as she slides gracefully from the breakfast nook. 'Are you coming?'

She's caught me with a mouth full of food again. I give her a thumbs-up and point to the food I'm still going to eat. I'm used to Sophie acting la-di-dah when Kate is around; I don't even try and join the club any more.

We eventually hit the road with the Lycra sisters sitting upfront and me and the giant pads (now tucked safely inside an opaque shopping bag) riding in the back of Kate's little car that smells of *Shake-'n'-Vac*. I don't know why but I'm feeling surprisingly cheery; I haven't thought about dying for at least an hour. It's strangely liberating to be around Sophie and Kate whose biggest dilemma is whether or not to give in to the carrot and mango smoothie. We park on the street and enter the gym's hallowed doors to find the place brimming with bulging biceps and sagging abs that together dream of streamlined perfection but will never be happy anyway.

'Shall we warm up on the treadmills?' Sophie asks Kate, who nods. Both girls look at me.

'I had better go and tell Misty I'm here. My father should be picking her up soon anyway,' I say.

'Oki koki,' Kate chirrups and immediately strides in the direction of the warm-up section. Sophie waves goodbye and chases after her. Oki koki? That headband is way too tight, my talking thoughts add their two pence.

I find Misty perched behind the counter of the gym's clothing shop called *Chic Shape*, paging through a copy of *Fit 'n' Fab* magazine. I can't actually see her face, but the magazine is balanced on an enormous pod belly that's hung with two curtains of fuzzy blonde hair.

'Misty,' I begin.

The magazine lowers slowly. Misty stares at me blankly for a few moments; I think she's trying to work out if she's Misty or if I'm the one introducing myself as

Misty. Which would be a coincidence, she's thinking. The front of her stretch T-shirt says GUESS? in long, distorted letters. Uh, pregnant? My talking thoughts have no self-control. Misty is a label junky who refuses to shop maternity.

'Oh, hello there,' she finally says. She remembers me.

'Hiya.' Awkward moment. 'I need a lift home with my father...Mackenzie...if that's OK.' I thought I'd better throw his name in there, to avoid any confusion.

'Oh. Right. OK then,' she smiles vaguely.

'When do you think he'll get here?' I ask.

Misty consults the digital diving watch on her wrist before replying. 'About five.'

Five minutes or five o' clock? I glance at my own wristwatch. She must mean five o' clock, which means I still have a twenty-minute wait. 'I'll go hang about with my friend until he gets here then,' I reply and offer up a thin smile.

'Oh, OK then.' That seems to be the end of the conversation so I U-turn and exit the shop. Misty and I are like aliens from different galaxies.

Kate and Sophie are still on the treadmills. Kate is striding hard and breathing like she's the one about to give birth while Sophie seems to be more interested in scoping out everyone around her.

'Hiya,' I say. Kate gives a quick salute to the headband and continues puffing determinedly. Sophie, on the other hand, doesn't seem terribly impressed to see me. I'm the only person here not dressed in shiny stretch-clothing. It's quite obvious I don't belong, and Sophie runs with the pack. Like it's my fault I have twenty empty minutes.

A woman with knotty runner's legs and abs like corrugated cardboard working the machine next to Sophie halts the treadmill and her stopwatch and springs lithely from the belt. Already feeling self-conscious and eager for something to do, I quickly claim the treadmill for my own and set it to a slow ambling speed. 'I'll keep you company, shall I?' I smile at my less-than-impressed friend.

'Go on then,' Sophie sighs and starts marching faster than before.

This treadmill business is for the birds – I'm not even breathing hard yet, so I increase my speed. 'I saw Misty in *Chic Shape*,' I say and laugh. 'I can just imagine her sitting there now, still trying to work out where she's seen me before. Ha ha.'

'I like Misty,' Sophie puffs.

'You've only met her…what, twice?' I say, not even bothering to strap a lead on my irritation. 'And she said what, like two words to you?'

Sophie sticks her chin out and increases her speed. 'So, I still like her.'

Supremely irritated by my friend's usual lack of support, I meet and then raise her a speed. 'And just what is it you like so much about her then?'

'I think she's sweet,' Sophie barks and meets and raises me a speed too.

'You know you only like her because I don't,' I huff, stretching my legs to keep up with the belt moving beneath my feet. That bit about me not liking Misty is not essentially true; we don't have any sort of relationship – good or bad (but then neither does Sophie, she's just very good at winding me up).

'Oh, whatever!' Sophie snaps and increases her speed yet again. Typical, she never knows when to stop.

Refusing to be beaten, I disregard my better judgement and move to increase my speed too. I'm now walking so fast my hips are rolling and my arms are swinging like I'm about to take off, which makes handling the treadmill's controls a bit of a hit-and-miss affair. Or in my case, a definite miss. I mistakenly jab the pause button and the black rubber floor goes from fifth gear to neutral in two unexpected seconds, literally pulling the belt out from under me and sending me sprawling face first. I land in a twisted tangle on the floor, shamefully and very publicly ejected from the assembly line of fit and fabulous keep-fit fanatics. I seem to have set aside this special time to humiliate myself in public.

It doesn't take Sophie very long to dismiss her treadmill, grab her workout towel and quickly stride as far away from my sorry self as she possibly can. Kate, on the other hand, seems more concerned with the fact that rolling about on the floor is most certainly against gym regulations, and she glowers at me and exhales through tunnel lips, like she's trying to put a fire out. It may be that my sole purpose in life is simply to serve as a warning to others.

Two significant things have taken place in the last week. The first is that there's now a small blue suitcase packed with clothes and a travel-size set of Misty's essentials waiting at the front door. My father took the time to explain to me that this means they're now fully prepared for the day when Misty starts having contractions and needs to be rushed to the hospital. He then went on about how I was not, under any circumstances, to touch the blue suitcase waiting at the front door. Boo hoo. There's one dream destroyed then, the thoughts tally.

The second significant thing is that I got another email from Sam, and he didn't refer to *that* email I sent him once. If he thinks I'm loop-the-loop, he hasn't mentioned it. He nattered on about trying out for his school hockey team, he asked how I was getting on with the flower sticks, he mentioned some film he had recently seen, and he said that Gloria had the flu but never fear because he was looking after her. No talk about my girly plumbing business though. I suppose this means I can breathe again and pretend that the mail malarkey never happened, but I still have no guarantees that Sam hasn't blabbed to Brighton. I did send Mum a mail which asked if she (or the rest of the south coast of England) had heard from Sam. She still hasn't replied though.

Today is Saturday morning and I'm holed up in my bedroom scribbling in my black doodlebook. I've been flitting between My Dying To Do List and my Last Will and Testament and added 'Go to church and ask forgiveness for my sins' to my Dying List. I've also left all my CDs to Sam; he deserves something for not making me feel like a pea head. I should probably also send him an email, or one that's intended for him anyway, considering that he's mailed me twice already. I've got my headphones on and I'm listening to a CD of dolphin calls accompanied by pan flutes. Mum gave it to me to help clear my head.

Hiya Sam,
Sorry that this is my FIRST email to you, I've been very busy at school and hanging out with all my friends. We just learnt in computer studies how hackers can tap into your email and send bogus emails from your address. Can you believe it!

It wouldn't surprise me if I was a victim of this kind of scam. I have bad luck like that. Anyway, sorry to hear about Gloria. I hope she gets better. I've been too busy for the flower sticks but I might give them a go this afternoon. And otherwise, life is great...parties, Butlins, dates to the movies...it's all go! If you see my mum please tell her that I love her and she owes me an email and a phone call.

Bye.

Libby

PS See you soon

I can hear my father and Misty working out on the landing. My father is doing his morning sit-ups and Misty is sitting on his ankles. She's also dressed in her workout gear, except she's in a lime two-piece that exposes her giant pod belly. In her defence, I don't think she could fit into anything else, which is exactly why I'm holed up in my bedroom. None of it is pretty.

Abandoning my Dying List and Will for the moment I turn my attention to the remembrance collage for the kid. I've saved a very special place in the middle of the collage for a postcard of my favourite picture in the entire world. It's a simple painting called *Mother and Child* by the artist Gustav Klimt, and it features a mother and her child naked, sleeping and beautiful. I adore it because the mother looks exactly like my own mum, before she cut off her long soft hair and bleached it as white as a goose. I also love it because the mother and child look so peaceful and vulnerable at the same time. They appear serene, wrapped up in sleep and protected by each other's love, and look like they'll stay that way forever – if the outside world can just butt out and leave them alone.

My father and Misty are getting louder and I have to turn up the volume on my CD player to camouflage their noise. The dolphin calls are now more of a screech, but it's still better than listening to 'one, two, squeeze…!' I'm sure the neighbours think we have bowel problems.

I glue the mother and child in their rightful place and draw small pale flowers – similar to the ones in the mother's hair – around the beautiful picture. I think I hear my name. I love this picture so much I think I'm experiencing some strange connection to it. It's almost like it's calling out to me, over and over.

'Liberty! Liberty!'

My father's tomato face is suddenly inches from my own. As it turns out he's the one calling me, not the picture. I think he's also responsible for pulling the plug on my headphones, because the dolphins have taken a dive.

'Liberty, would you snap out of it! Misty has gone into labour and I'm rushing her to the hospital. You need to stay here.' His hands are cutting the air like he's directing traffic. I jump out of my chair and stand quietly to attention. So the kid's finally coming then, my talking thoughts muse with interest. Suddenly the air vibrates with a long and plaintive howl. I can only presume that Misty and her lungs had something to do with that. 'We must all stay calm!' my father shouts. And you're telling me this? 'I will phone you from the hospital.' He does a 180-degree turn on the heel of his trainer and marches in the direction of the wailing, but then pauses at the door for one final parting statement.

'And for goodness sake Liberty, get out of those pyjamas!' It's not his fault, he can't help himself. Giving orders is what he does.

I stand there listening to the sounds of my father assisting a grunting Misty and her gigantic pod belly down the stairs and out of the front door, which slams shut, opens again and then once again slams shut. Somebody almost forgot the blue suitcase. I would've helped them but my father makes it impossible. I'd only get in his way.

The squeal of tyres follows his Audi down the road. I'm in the newly decorated nursery by the time it finally disappears. Everything in this room is creamy and fresh and optimistic. The kid with his or her brand new baby body and soul will hang out in this room and grow and learn a little bit more every single day, and before long the Winnie the Pooh mural and musical mobiles will be replaced by dirt bikes or Malibu Barbie or whatever else the kid is into. That'll be followed by pop music and crushes, or dumb-bells and posters of bodybuilders (you can't always fight the genes), and then it'll be university or whatever else the kid decides to do with his or her life. But this room is where it will all begin. The kid is starting and I'm ending.

Thomas Mackenzie Belle came into this world roaring like a pro-wrestler. He's apparently got black hair and brown eyes and according to my father, he's a definite heavyweight. I wouldn't personally refer to a newborn baby in World Wrestling Federation terms, but considering that I haven't seen my brother yet I have nothing else to go on. My father felt that Misty would prefer it if we gave her a bit of time and space to adjust to motherhood first, but I think he means if I gave her a bit of time, because he's at the hospital every chance he gets. Still, Misty and Thomas (call him Tommy and watch my father's eyes catch fire) will be there when I get home from school this afternoon. And I only have a few days to bond with him before I head off to Brighton to stay with Mum for the school holidays. I wish I had a bit more time with Tommy (this is going to be fun), but being with Mum is the bigger deal. That's called life.

My father's car is in the driveway, which means that they're home already. My palms are hot and leaky;

I think I'm suddenly nervous. I suppose I shouldn't underestimate this momentous event. I'm sure Tom and I will get along just fine – we have, after all, taken a dip in the same gene pool, or half of us has anyway. And I am his big sister. Of course we'll get along. I open the front door to find Misty on the couch cradling a very small human in her arms and my father looking down on the pair of them like they've just descended directly from heaven. He hears me enter and glances up; his eyes are dreamy and glistening. He looks like he's having a spiritual experience.

'Hiya,' is my general blanket greeting.

'Liberty, come and meet your baby brother!' my father cries out with cheeks that are as bright and shiny as Christmas tree ornaments. I quietly drop my schoolbag on the carpet and sidle over to the space in front of the couch beside my father. 'Go on,' he urges me excitedly.

I bend to inspect the little fella and notice that Misty just happens to be breastfeeding. Not only am I about to get my first glorious glimpse of my darling baby brother, but I'm also going to get a very large eyeful of Misty's great white breast. We've barely progressed past a casual hello and now I'm staring at her boobage. I must try and concentrate on the tiny thatched head sticking out of the buttercup blanket instead.

I crouch lower and slide my fingers through his black hair which is as soft as the fur on a kitten's belly. I can feel his spongy skull through his warm silky scalp; he'd definitely break if you dropped him. His tiny pudgy face is red and wrinkled, like a little old man with too much whiskey in him. I watch his pale creased lips frantically sucking like a pond fish coming up for air. His forehead is furrowed in concentration; he doesn't want to miss a drop. He's so delicate and determined and exquisite and I feel something inside me stir, like a butterfly that's emerged from a chrysalis and opened its wings for the very first time – tickling me between my ribs. That's when I know that I love him already.

'He's beautiful,' I congratulate the angels that got him here safely. I look from my brother to the boob to Misty, who for the first time actually seems to acknowledge my presence.

'Thomas Belle – our little miracle,' she smiles, and for the first time ever I wonder if we actually have a chance at being some sort of normal family.

'Thomas Mackenzie Belle,' my father corrects her. 'We're having him christened next week; Misty's parents are driving here all the way from Devon on Saturday.'

'You're having him christened next week?' I cry. 'But I won't be here.'

My father looks at me for a few moments and then releases a long breathy sigh. 'You decided to go to Brighton, Liberty. Misty's parents leave next week for their round-the-world cruise, you know that. And we want Thomas christened before his first birthday. So it's out of our hands.'

Actually, I didn't know about Misty's parents or their cruise or anything, for that matter. And so what if they're travelling around the world? They may be Tommy's grandparents but I'm his sister – half or not, I should count too. Misty is shushing Thomas and rocking him gently like he's kicking up a fuss, except he looks fast asleep to me.

'You're going to upset the baby,' my father frowns.

'Yeah, well I'm not exactly doing cartwheels myself.' This time my talking thoughts have broken free.

'Don't get stroppy with me,' he orders. 'And don't ruin what should be a very happy day for all of us.'

Yes, as long as I tow the line and slot quietly into your life then it will be a happy day. You think that I should just be grateful and do my best to fit in with your family – the family that used to be you and Mum and me and then became you and Misty and now includes a baby called Thomas. Did you ever stop to think what I might feel like? That I might have lost my place in the world? You and Mum decided to put an end to the life we shared together, but you've left me with nothing in its place.

'I suppose they'll be staying in my room then?' I say instead, referring to Misty's world-cruising parents.

'Of course they will, where else?' my father snorts.

'And were you even going to tell me?'

'What difference does it make? And besides, I say what goes on in my house.' His eyeballs flick subconsciously toward the couch and I realise that even though this row is between my father and me, he's representing Misty and himself and *their* house. That's how it is now, I suppose. They're married and I'm a cling-on – a reminder of the past he was desperate to escape from.

Standing there in the lounge I can feel their eyes hot on me and I suddenly feel very self-conscious, like I'm one of those pesky relatives who always makes a scene and ruins what could otherwise be a very pleasant family gathering. I silently retrieve my bag and head upstairs to my room, the one I share with Misty's world-cruising parents. I don't actually have a problem with them staying in my room, but I would have liked to have been told. I'm not a child any more; I'm actually a young woman now, even if both my parents are oblivious to the fact.

Email is my great escape. I still haven't heard from

Mum but Sam has already replied to my email. He filled me in on his school and asked about my friends (including the male variety), but he didn't mention a word about the so-called hackers that tap into people's email addresses. Reading his email through for a second time makes me wish I hadn't tried to sound so cool in my last mail. One particular line of his message keeps repeating over and over in my head, making me feel like a big, fat fraud:

You sound like you have a very busy social life, Libby. I wish I could say the same...you might not think so – but I'm a bit of a shy one.

It takes courage to lay yourself open and expose your insecurities like that. I remember reading somewhere that it's better to be disliked for what you are than to be loved for what you are not (maybe the Dalai Lama said that too?). Finally I meet someone just like me, somebody who's not as hip and happening as the rest of the world, and all I do is put on an act. I suck. But it's not too late...

Hiya Sam,
Oh, my social life is not as busy as all that. I have friends with great social lives though, does that

count? Ha ha. And in answer to your question, no I don't have a boyfriend. I don't really even have any boy friends (spot the difference) either. I go to an all-girls' school and pretty much nowhere else. I have a new baby brother called Thomas though. He's really beautiful. Have you seen my mum around? How is she doing?

See you soon.

Libby

I spend the following day thinking about Tommy instead of my schoolwork. I even attempt to tell Sophie what a good baby he is but she's being very cool towards me since the treadmill incident. Still, it's just as well I didn't brag too much because when I finally get home, Tommy spends the rest of the afternoon howling. He keeps my father and Misty very busy and gives me a big, fat headache. Eventually my father makes some excuse about having to put in a few hours at the office while Misty moans that she's going to pass out if she doesn't get some sleep, which is how I finally get some alone-time with the kid. He stares up at me from his Winnie the Pooh swaddling and smiles if I do really stupid things with my face and whimpers when I don't, which is fairly exhausting after the first ten seconds. I was hoping for some soulful bonding time, but perhaps this *is* soulful bonding to a newborn baby.

I already made the decision to give Pippen the toy possum to Tommy a while ago. It would have been number four of my Last Will and Testament, but I've now decided to give it to him as an early christening gift instead. My nana made Pippen for my mum many, many years ago, but he's still in quite good condition. His brown knitted possum body is still plump and smooth, he's only lost the felt off one of his paws, he has both button eyes and his stitched-cotton mouth still has its friendly smile. And now is as good a time as any, so I hand Pippen over to Tommy and carefully explain that I have a very good reason for not making his christening. I tell him that he'll understand one day and he seems to take the disappointing news in his stride. I think he's like me in that way.

Misty wakes up for Tommy's feed and my father eventually slouches in from the office, which means I'm now back in my bedroom and using the peaceful silence to tackle my homework. Or I was, until my email Inbox flashed with a new message from Sam. I click to open.

Congratulations, new big sister! I hope he's got your good looks! :-) I don't have a girlfriend either, or

many girl friends (spot the difference) for that matter. You're my first (girl friend). As for your mum, sorry Libby – I haven't seen her since her birthday. I asked Gloria though, and she says Iris is doing a lot of work at a centre called Sumskiri Khuki or something (don't ask me). You'll be seeing her soon, so try not to worry. Hey, show the new tot your flower sticks and tell him all about your spot-the-difference boy friend Sam. ;-) Babies dig me!

C u in a few days,

The Sameister

Tommy may have stopped crying but it's my father and Misty making the noise now. If I didn't know any better I'd think they were arguing, but they never argue, or not when I'm around anyway. And that's exactly what I tell Mum when she asks.

'I just don't want it in here,' I hear Misty say. Her voice is louder than before.

'What harm can it do?' my father hisses in a low, hoarse voice. He's annoyed, but he's trying to keep quiet about it.

'It's old and disgusting, for a start.'

'We'll wash it then,' he strains.

'It's ugly too.'

'It's a stuffed toy for goodness sake, not a piece of art.'

'And it doesn't go with the room.'

'I doubt the baby will notice.' My father is starting to lose his grip.

'Mackenzie, I don't need this! Do you know what it's like to survive on three hours of sleep a day and then have something sucking on you and needing you and demanding things from you? I look disgusting. I feel even worse. And now you expect me to have your ex-wife's childhood toys in our baby's nursery. For-get it!' That's the most we've ever heard Misty say in one go, my talking thoughts are the first to notice.

A door slams and Tommy starts crying loudly. You don't need superior intelligence to work out that Pippin the possum has brought trouble and strife to the happy family. I don't move or breathe. This latest turn of events doesn't make me nearly as happy as I thought it would. In fact, it doesn't make me happy at all. I just feel a bit embarrassed really. I'm still that pesky relative who, once again, has upset the happy family.

And maybe that's just it – they are a family. And this is their home, not mine. My father and Misty chose this house and all its brand new furniture together. Brand new meant no memories of the past, although I did get to bring a couple of boxes of my own things. Still, if this was my home I'd be able to do things like keep my bedroom door closed and paint the walls something other than white. It would be OK to settle into the sofa and eat the biscuit tin empty or invite friends to visit without asking permission in advance. And I'd be entitled to give Thomas a gift that meant something to me, because this would be my home and my brother and my right too. When I visit Mum's I don't have to wash a dish the very instant I'm done with it. I can laugh out loud like a fool and not hear 'ssh'. When I'm at Mum's I fit in, I'm just plain old Libby, not some stranger. This is my address, not my home. And I can't see how it ever will be.

It's this dreary train of thought that finally leads me to a somewhat sunnier destination. This is when it comes to me. I've just had a life-changing revelation. Yes, I believe I finally have it all worked out. I am going to ask Mum if I can live with her instead! If I stay with Mum my father will have to pay her maintenance. And maintenance means money – and quite a bit of it, I suppose. Why didn't I think of this before! The problem has been solved – Mum and I can finally live together and be our own stable little family...well, until I die, that is. But at least we'll get some quality time in before then. Sure, I'll nip off to visit my father and

Tommy (depending on how much time I have left, of course). But that will be up to me. I bet my father and the Pippen-hater will be a whole lot nicer to me then. I realise that living with Mum means I'll have to endure her soya spaghetti and rice drink, but who cares! And sure, I'll have to give up my bedroom (the one I share with Misty's ocean-cruising parents) and make do with the futon in Mum's dining room, but I'm sure I can do it up and make it my own. I'm thinking – and I can already picture it: a seaside theme. That way Mum will still get some use out of the room when I catch that travellator into the sky. Of course I'll have to change schools but that's OK too – I don't much like my school…can't stomach the place really. Two birds and all of that. Woo hoo! Ha, I bet Sophie is going to wish she'd been a bit nicer to me too. Yes, I've given it some thought and I think I've got it all worked out already. The next step in my plan is to arrange the finer details with Mum.

Part Two
The Renaissance
(well, sort of)

twelve
strengthening my resolve

My cap is pulled down low enough to screen my drifting eyes, providing me with some perfect peeking prospects. Dark sunglasses are the ultimate staring accessory (you don't even have to pretend not to), but for now my cap will have to do.

There's a woman as tall as a man with big blonde hair sitting one aisle across from me who has been emptying beer cansinto her mouth since the train left Manchester station, and she's growing louder and happier with each one. Up until now she's managed to limit herself to shiny-eyed sweeping surveys of her surroundings accompanied by sporadic giggles, but I've been watching her eyeballing the young woman with her head wrapped up in a pink swirled scarf sitting in the seat across from her. She's been giving her 'best-friend' grins for the last ten minutes and is quite obviously bursting for some jovial conversation. It's only a matter of time.

'My name is Rutha,' she finally explodes in a gravely accent that could be Russian. She rolls the 'r' off her palate like a purring cat and irrigates the table separating her from her new best friend with beer flavoured spittle. 'I am from Latvia!' she declares, extending her hand in the universal gesture of friendship.

The young woman with the pink swirled head seems unfazed and offers her small hand up with a smile. ''Ello, I am Juliette.' But it sounds more like 'Shoolytte', so she might be French. 'And I am from France.' Score! Nobody in England is from England any more; I'm a master at this train game.

'Ooooh!' Rutha exclaims and then blabbers something that's completely unintelligible. Now she's staring at Juliette expectantly.

'Pardon?' the young woman finally asks.

'Don't you speak French?' Rutha slurs.

'I am French.'

'But do you *speak* French?' Rutha is getting impatient now.

'Oui! But of course,' Juliette smiles tolerantly.

Rutha siphons another garbled sentence through her rubbery lips and then once again stares at Juliette expectantly. Her blue eyes are large and wet and blinking frantically and she has a manic grin on her face. Juliette, on the other hand, is starting to look nervous. She was only trying to be nice and now she's got to decipher at least five beer cans' worth of French with a Latvian accent before she has any hope of returning to the book laying abandoned in her lap.

'Say it for me!' Rutha demands, still grinning.

Juliette may be small but she's not silly and even though she has zero idea exactly what it is Rutha wants her to say, she lifts her chin in the air defiantly and suddenly spews forth about who-knows-what (I don't speak the language either). Still, it sounds very pretty and rather a lot like French. She then pauses while the train travellers within earshot simultaneously lean one millimetre forward in their seats. And just when we all think the show's over, Juliette starts babbling something else. She's conveniently forgotten how to speak English and finally concludes her speech with a coy smile. She hasn't taken her eyes off the stunned lady from Latvia once and is now clearly relishing her turn to look expectant.

Rutha's face suddenly slips from friendly and fun to distrustful and dour; she has no idea what Juliette has just said, but there's one thing she's very sure of: she's one Latvian lady who *can speak French!*

'Pah!' she grunts dismissively. Her tongue still looks loose but Juliette is braced to go another round so Rutha remains quiet and stares at her suspiciously, now properly convinced that she's being duped. The girl in the pink swirled headscarf must be quite mad, she finally decides with a scowl and an unsteady shake of her head. But who cares, she can always find another best friend. She grabs her handbag and staggers to her feet, staring hard at the ground in front of her and muttering softly.

All of the eavesdroppers – myself included – almost bust a chin snapping our heads to our chests. And we've all fallen instantly asleep. Now more suspicious than ever, Rutha zigzags her way down the aisle and through the concertina doors, never to return again. It's the conductor who eventually comes to retrieve the bag she stowed in the overhead compartment, but by then I barely even notice. I'm too busy staring out of the train window at the Brighton station platform, where Sam is standing and chattering away to my mum whose hair is still as white and glistening as a goose.

'Hi darling!' Mum spies me first.

Hi yourself, Sumskiri-seriously-Kooky non-emailing person, my talking thoughts scowl.

'Hey Liberty,' Sam smiles at me. I forgot all about his eyes. They're still different colours, like two bright gemstones catching the light.

'Uh, hey Sam.' I still haven't forgotten about *that* email, even if he's pretending he has, and I watch him carefully and try to work out if he's mocking me.

'How was your trip?' he asks sincerely.

'Necessary I suppose.' Train trips are what you do when your mother has deserted you for a seaside hippy commune.

'Are you all right, darling?' Mum asks, running her hands over my head like I'm four and my hair is still damp from washing.

'I suppose I have my health,' I reply and swat her hands from my head. I'm an emotional train wreck though. And who knows just how long I'll have my health for. Maybe I should tell her that I'll be dying soon.

'Aurora is parked around the corner,' Mum changes the subject. 'You must be starving. Gloria invited us around for lunch today,' she adds. 'That's OK with you, isn't it?'

'Ha, except I'm pretty sure that Mick will end up doing the cooking. As usual!' Sam pipes up. 'Spaghetti bolognaise with soya, mmm.' He grins and gives me a secret wink, although I'm focusing on my mum, who for some reason appears slightly flustered. I don't know why she thinks I'd mind going to Gloria and Sam's for lunch. In fact, hearing that Mick is going to be there and cooking is very good news indeed. I must have it all wrong; dear old affectionate Mick must be Gloria's boyfriend or husband or life partner, or whatever they call it these days. He's quite obviously just my mum's *boy friend*. Spot the difference.

'Cool,' I smile. I'm feeling better already.

Sam, Gloria and Mick live a short drive from the station and I update Mum and Sam on baby Tommy along the way, but I don't mention his christening or Pippen either and it's not long before Sam points to the house he shares with Gloria and Mick. They live in a narrow two-storey terrace at the end of a side street that's so skinny it could pass for an alleyway. Aurora negotiates the curbs while I mentally fret over Mum's atrocious park-by-ear driving skills, and soon we're out in the sunshine and heading for the front door with its round portal window decorated with a stained glass fairy. The dainty bamboo windchime dangling from the overhead light is tinkling in the Brighton breeze. I sniff happily at its saltiness. I have six endless weeks stretched out before me. I have stepped out of the shadows and I feel liberated and delirious and hopeful, like anything is possible – even living with my mum again.

Gloria appears to welcome us at the door and as she takes both my hands, I realise that this is the first time we've actually been introduced. She's quite a bit older than my mum and still looks absolutely nothing like her son. Sam must resemble his father, who I'm almost sure is not Mick.

'Hello Liberty! How brilliant to finally meet you face to face,' she says. Her voice is as soft and sweet as a marshmallow; this woman should narrate children's stories. Her wispy strawberry-blonde hair is pulled away from her face with two shell clips and her features are as delicate and pointed as the fairy on her front door.

'Nice to meet you too,' I smile politely.

We all traipse inside and give our eyes a few moments to open up to the shade. This house is colourful and almost cluttered compared with Mum and Lotus's minimalist cottage. I like it immediately. It's cosy and homely and full of scattered clues about the people who live here. Almost every surface has at least one painted fairy perched on it – a passion of Gloria's (I'm hoping). The right wall is broken with a row of framed photographs of Sam in his velvet jester hat juggling colourful balls, flower sticks and what could be fresh fruit. My father would call that playing with your food. Near a window stands an easel holding a stretched canvas covered in a pencil outline and the pale painted legs and turquoise tulip skirt of what will probably turn out to be a fairy. I don't see a box of paints anywhere, but there's a battered skateboard tipped on its side trapped between the easel's stick legs. I don't see many signs of Mick around the place either. Perhaps he's the minimalist one.

Mum disappears into the kitchen with Gloria, leaving Sam and I alone. 'I'm going to get a drink, would you like one too?' he asks.

'No thanks,' I reply and occupy myself with the photographs standing on a side bureau. The frames are all different but the pictures are of the same young man with pale hair and fine bones. One of the photos shows him dressed up in a brown soldier's uniform. He's got a gun slung uncomfortably across his shoulders and if the look on his face says anything, it's that he doesn't have much faith in the safety catch.

'Are you ready to eat?' Mum appears and hooks her fingers with mine.

'Sure,' I smile.

'Well, come on, we're eating al fresco today.'

I follow her through the kitchen and out of the back door to a small garden that's governed by a dressed wooden table and Mick wearing his denim hot pants with frayed hems. At least he's left the Stetson hat upstairs this time.

'You remember Mick, don't you?' Mum asks hopefully.

'Sure, hiya,' I nod. How could we forget? But as long

as Gloria likes the shorts then that's all that matters, I remind my talking thoughts to play nicely.

Mick greets me and returns to the garden salad he's expertly tossing in a bowl. 'Sit sit,' Gloria urges me into a chair and ceremoniously lowers a plate full of steaming bolognaise down in front of me.

'Thanks,' I smile, 'it smells great.' I aim that last bit at Mick, just to prove that there are no hard feelings and even though I still believe he could be a little more subtle with his crotch area, it really is a free world.

Everyone takes their place and Mick says a prayer of thanks for the food, the beautiful day and each other, but no one closes their eyes and they all stare up at the sky instead, so I do the same. And then we're off – eating and talking and laughing and having a pretty good time. I'm sitting in between Gloria and Sam and they keep me busy with questions and interesting stories about themselves. Even the soya spaghetti is good and I'm having such a great time I don't even give dying a single thought.

'I forgot the garlic bread!' Mum suddenly cries out and jumps to her feet.

Mick is quick to follow. 'You enjoy your meal, I'll fetch it,' he announces, determined to save the day. But he doesn't dash off straightaway. First he cups Mum's chin in his hand. Then he mashes his lips against hers. Finally he gives her bottom an exuberant slap before disappearing indoors.

Everyone else is suddenly very still and silent – everyone except for me, that is. I just happen to be halfway through a large mouthful of spag-bol and the shock of seeing Chicken Mick smooching my mother and then slapping her rear end grabs me by the throat and squeezes hard, forcing the spaghetti that was halfway down my gullet to shoot straight back up and out through my nose with a loud snort. And it all happens so quickly I don't even realise I have spaghetti dangling from my nostrils until I reach Gloria's bathroom.

It's not the smooth round pebbles that are making walking difficult, it's the awkward gradient of their slope – the end result of the continual raking back and forth, dawn to dusk, of the ocean's tides. The whip of the wind has left my bare feet sticky and frozen, but that's the least of my worries. I don't even mind the short sharp slaps of cold against the exposed sliver of my belly that's got the short end of my T-shirt. None of that matters right now.

'You should have told me.' I frown at the horizon.

'I was going to,' Mum replies, 'but I was waiting for the right time and then of course poor Mick forgot himself and well…we never meant to hurt you, Libby.'

There's that *we* again; everybody seems to be part of a 'we' these days. My father's 'we' is Misty and him, and now my mother has Chicken Mick. So which comfy little circle do I fit into then? Am I part of a 'we' too?

'I don't know what you see in a grown man who walks around in denim hot pants anyway,' I scowl meanly. I glance up to catch the impact of my words on her face.

I want to see her hurt; why else would I say it? Mum flinches and sets her jaw rigidly but doesn't respond. 'And as for that stupid Stetson hat he wears, where does he think he is – the Wild West?'

'I think you need to cool it, Libby.'

'Mick with his chicken legs,' I rage against the wind and my mum's new boyfriend, determined to push my luck as far as possible because that will be the measure of how much she loves me more than him. 'Mick and his stupid chicken legs and daft cowboy hat! That's why I call him Mr Kentucky Fried Chicken, you know. That or Chicken Mick, depending on how bothered I can be.'

'Don't push it, Lib,' Mum says quietly.

'So what is he – some weirdo tarot reader who goes about in Roman sandals and lives in a tepee then?' I keep on pushing.

'He lives in a house, he's a builder by trade and we work together at the Centre for Sumskiri Khuki.'

'Well, that explains why you spend your life there and I don't even get so much as an email then!' I knew the Kooky Centre had something to do with this. Oh, and by the way, I don't actually want to know a single thing about him, thanks very much. I'm right here and yet all you can do is talk about him. But I don't let my vent go beyond my talking thoughts; I don't want her to know that I feel threatened by him, just in case it makes him sound more significant than he really is. She's lonely and he's a phase. Once I'm living with her she'll feel differently. Now is a good time to let Mum in on my maintenance plan.

'I wasn't keeping secrets from you, Libby,' she speaks first. 'I just didn't know if this thing with Mick was serious or not. I wanted to tell you once I was sure, and well…I guess now you know.'

'So what, you're telling me that this thing with Chick…with Mick is serious then?'

'We care about each other a great deal,' she nods.

'For just how long have you been together?'

'I've known Mick for about a year actually, but we've only been uh…a couple for the last few months.'

A *couple?* Oh spare me the sordid details! My parents seem to have forgotten that they're supposed to be the sedate adults and *I'm* the randy teenager around here. Or I'm supposed to be, anyway. My life is upside down.

'Just don't tell me you're thinking of getting married again too,' I fume, not for one moment actually considering that she ever would. Mum swore she would never walk down the aisle again.

'No,' she replies, shaking her head, 'but we have

spoken about moving in together. Not now, but who knows, one day soon maybe.'

Living together? But you can't, because you and I are going to live together, just as soon as I tell you about the maintenance plan I have worked out! Mum's the only one who understands me but she's moving forward and leaving me far behind.

She stops walking and snatches my hand. 'Just give Mick a chance,' she says gently, ducking and diving to catch my eyes. 'He's a nice man, Libby.'

I stare hard at the smooth, mottled pebbles rolling beneath my toes, which I've also painted with pretty pink flowers. Like the fact that I'm finally a woman, my painted toes are another thing Mum hasn't even noticed. I'm nice too, I want to say but don't. And I used to be your wonderful, perfect daughter, only now I'm dying.

Like an instant and direct connection to all the right answers, I suddenly realise that I will never have my old family – *my* family – back again. My father and Misty have their new family, and Mum and Mick will have theirs, and I'll move between the two – never quite belonging to either one; the odd one out, the remnant from the past they're all trying so desperately to escape from.

Mum interprets my silence as sullenness and attempts

to steer our conversation to smooth, shallower waters. 'So you're a big sister then, huh! That's pretty cool,' she grins and rubs my head affectionately.

'Yeah, it's pretty cool,' I echo softly.

'You're happy living in Manchester, aren't you, Libby.' But it sounds less like a question and more like an observation she's making, as if she's hoping to convince me with the answer she most wants to hear. And there's no *Excellent Work!* gold star for guessing why it's her favourite answer either. Chicken Mick has probably already got his stuff packed and I sorely doubt that a moody teenager crashing on the futon in the dining room is quite what he signed up for. But that's fine, because I'm not into collecting strays either.

'Oh, Manchester is great.' I side-step the truth. I suppose I shouldn't really be upset. After all, what's the point in asking Mum if I can come and live with her when I'm going to be dying soon. I'm not going to be around for much longer anyway. It's hardly worth the move.

'I was such a young mum, Libby,' Mum finally says with a small smile that's close to breaking in two. 'I was practically a kid myself and everything just happened so quickly. But I need you to understand where I'm at in my life now. I'm only thirty-three years old and just like you, there's still so much ahead of me. Of course it's sad that your father and I were incompatible, but you've always brought us the greatest joy imaginable. You made everything…all those years…worthwhile. Your father and I were never meant to be, but you certainly were. All I'm asking Libs, is for you to just please give me a chance too. Nothing will ever change my love for you, OK? I promise you that.'

I remain silent and unmoving and let her words wash over me like the cold grey water rinsing the pebbles on the beach. I let their meaning seep through my layers, bubbling deeper and deeper. But still I don't say anything.

'You know what I think?' she finally asks.

'What?'

'I think we should buy you an open annual train ticket so that you can visit as often as you like – whenever you like. I should have a bit of spare cash soon, so how about it?' she elbows me playfully.

I switch from the pebbles to my mum's face, which is bright and glowing with buoyant cheeriness. She's grinning like a jackpot winner. This is her bit of big news; she's been working up to this.

Yes, my talking thoughts take a stab at optimism, an open train ticket should be fine. That should make everything better.

'You know what else we need?' Mum asks.

'What?'

'We need some retail therapy. Let's go and buy you something nice.'

'Something nice?' Right now *nice* is not what I need.

'Yes, I think the time has come for us to go bra shopping.'

'Oh please, I have bras already.'

'They're boring old training bras. I'm talking about pretty proper ones; I think you're about ready.'

I can't believe my own mother is gawking at my chest. 'Fine, whatever,' I nod self-consciously. Agreeing is the quickest way to get us moving along.

The nearest shopping mall is only a walk away but we hop into Aurora and make it there within minutes. I'm not in the mood for shopping or acting cheery. I'm still trying to come to terms with the fact that not only does my mother have a boyfriend, but she thinks that it's serious. Mum, on the other hand, is brimming with so much gusto I can barely keep up with her. Even if I wanted to.

'What do you think of this, Libby?' She has a purple skirt in her hands.

'Funny looking bra,' I smart-mouth.

'We'll look for bras in a minute, but we might as well

see what else there is while we're here. Hey, look at this gorgeous top! I love the embroidered butterflies.'

'Mmm.'

'Oh and look, it has a matching belt.'

'Right.'

'Hold on, I think we've found it – this dress is perfect for you!' It has a zip all the way down the back; I don't do zippy dresses. I stare at Mum blankly, but she holds it up against me anyway. 'The colour is just right too.'

'It's strawberry.'

'It's sherbet pink – very fashionable. And besides, you need some colour in your wardrobe.' The fight has left me and we take the dress and head for the underwear section. Mum is immediately drawn to the flowers, frills and bows. 'We really should have you measured up for your right size, just to be certain,' she declares authoritatively, casually sizing up my chest for the second time today. Anybody watching us would think we had these mother-daughter outings every other day.

'I don't think so.' I stomp on that idea and reach for something plain, white and cotton.

'While we're out shopping, is there anything else you need? Maybe we should get you more sanitary towels, you know – just in case?' That suggestion came in from the left field.

'Too late.' I say this so carelessly it's an accusation. 'Sophie had to give me more already.'

'She did? You have! Congratulations, my darling.' She grins and makes a grab for me with hug-shaped arms.

'Yeah, well, that was a while ago,' I step out of reach.

'It was?' Mum looks a little distressed. 'When? Why didn't you tell me?'

'Oh I tried, but you weren't there to answer my call or email.'

'You know I'm no good with computers, Libby.'

'Well, I'm sorry Mum, but my telepathic skills were down on that particular day. The telephone and email were the only ways I had of contacting you all the way down in Brighton. Perhaps you should give me the number of the Kooky Centre, I might have better luck reaching you there.'

'Don't be like that, Libs,' Mum groans. 'I'm so sorry – I never knew.'

'No, you didn't. Paint me surprised.'

The blonde-haired, blue-eyed mother and daughter pair cruising the underwear display beside us give me goggle eyes. I wish I had the nerve to tell them to mind their own snooty beeswax. I'd like to say a few more things to my preoccupied mother too. I'd like to tell her that things probably won't be any different when I have my first proper kiss, or get a boyfriend or boobage, or when I one day decide to lose my virginity. She lives in Brighton while I live in Manchester, that's just how it is. We can send endless emails and make all the promises in the world, but absolutely nothing will change the fact that she's now a long-distance mum. And it wouldn't be quite so bad if I had the sort of father I could talk to, but as it stands, I'm flying my teenage years solo. So it's just as well I'm checking out of this planet soon. In fact, I'm quite relieved.

I would say all of these things, but the blonde mother and daughter are still staring. I pull a tongue at the girl and she scurries closer to her mother and whispers something conspiratorially under her breath. Yes, run to Mummy, I glare at her back.

'I know you don't see it now, Libby, but one day you'll realise that this is for the best,' Mum stammers. 'Your father can provide the stability and security I just can't offer you right now. I spent the last decade raising you; I never finished university and I've never had a career so I've had to start at the bottom. I work long hours to pay the bills. And it's not just about the money or the overtime, it's about you being raised in a proper family environment and having all the things your friends have. I want you to have as normal a life as possible. You wouldn't have that here. I know you don't see it now but maybe one day you will. And maybe someday – when I've found my feet, we can talk about you living here with me in Brighton more of the time.'

Even if I had some hope for the future, someday is not even a day of the week. 'That doesn't help me very much right now though, does it?' I whisper just loud enough to be heard.

Mum's mouth turns soft and sad-shaped and the light in her eyes brightens with understanding. Her pupils dart left and right, searching my own, looking for more clues and insights into my teenage mind. She's been nurturing all of these grand plans for the future, but perhaps she finally realises that tomorrow is not enough to see me through. Tomorrow is just pie in the sky when you're thirteen and lost and surviving from one day to the next.

'Just how did we get to this point, Libby?' she finally sighs miserably. 'I've left you to work out too much for yourself, I realise that. I just wish I had more of the answers. I am so sorry, sweetheart. I'm the adult and your mother; I should be the one anticipating the events in your life – big and small. And I should be better prepared and there for you *all* of the time – especially now that I'm...well, living here. But I *can* be there for you, I promise. I've taken it for granted that you're happy and settled and coping with this arrangement. I've presumed too much. I'm not perfect, but I will change. And you know what we're going to do, right now, this very minute?'

My face is empty and unmoving. I'm not feeling optimistic, but Mum doesn't seem put off.

'We are going to buy two mobile phones – one for each of us.' She's watching my face for a reaction. She's still not getting one. 'They'll come with a strict set of rules, too!' she charges ahead excitedly. 'Our phones must *always* be fully charged. And we must carry them around with us every single moment of the day. They'll be like our own personal walkie-talkies. I'll make sure that we never run out of credit. Oh, and we'll text every day – every hour if we want to! We'll be there for each other – just a phone call away, twenty-four-seven.' Mum is smiling and looking at me, still searching for my reaction to this magnificent solution to all our problems.

Walkie-talkies? Sometimes I think my mum's more old age than New Age. Still, I suppose knowing that she's just a guaranteed phone call or text away will help things slightly. That and the open train ticket. I know she doesn't have very much money, so she really must be determined to make this work. That means something too. I keep my feelings hidden from my face though.

'Whenever and whatever you need – that will always be my priority. You are my priority, Libby. Now and always.' Mum's enthusiasm has nowhere else to go and finally seems to be slowing. 'I'm so sorry if I haven't been showing it. Will you give me another chance?'

A part of me wants her to feel bad, just to make sure that she hurts like I do. Why should I make this easy on her? I turn away and stare at the wire branches of dangling knickers and bras surrounding me like a forest of frills. This really is a crazy place to be having this discussion. I wonder where the bonded blonde mother and daughter pair are. Probably having a cosy cuddle somewhere. Or pointing and giggling at the lacy lingerie. They look the type. Finally I have what I've always wanted, my mother's undivided attention, and now I'm not sure what to do with it.

'Please?' She looks like she'd give anything.

I shrug and nod at the same time.

'This won't necessarily be forever,' she then adds, sensing my ambivalence.

But if I die one day soon, like I'm pretty sure I'm going to, then it will be forever. I don't say this out loud though.

'Living between Manchester and Brighton can't be

easy on you.' She runs her fingers through my hair thoughtfully, like all of this just occurred to her. 'But life isn't always easy, Libs…things don't always go the way we'd hoped. But we can try our best to make this as good as it can possibly be. I promise you that I will.'

If I open my mouth I might scream or cry – I'm not sure which, so I pick up a giant pair of polyester granny-pants, hold it up against me and laugh manically instead.

fourteen
living the dream

Today Mum has to work a full day at the Kooky Centre so Sam has offered to take me on a day trip around Brighton. I like Sam, he's happy and uncomplicated. I like Brighton too, it's carefree and exciting. We've made a late start but we're finally on the bus heading down to the beach front.

'That's the Royal Pavilion,' Sam says, aiming a finger at the billowing, putty coloured building with its Indian domes and pointed minarets stabbing the sky. 'It was a seaside palace, once upon a time. You should see the inside, it's done up Chinese style with fancy dragons and carved palm trees and fake bamboo staircases.'

Sam is relishing his role as tour guide and I don't have the heart to tell him that I've passed this building before and I still think it looks out of place in an English seaside town. Even my talking thoughts are keeping quiet for a change. He's wearing the same beige cargo shorts he wore the first day we met outside Earthly Delights, except today he's accessorised it with a T-shirt in a deep shade of blue that falls somewhere between the two colours of his eyes. He's also left the jester hat at home, thank goodness – although he only wears the jester hat when he's juggling, he's already told me a hundred times over.

He leans over to point out St Peter's Church, flavouring the air I'm breathing with his nearness. He has a comforting sort of smell – a bit like Christmas spice. I don't think he's brushed his hair this morning and his thick, soft curls are clearly doing their own thing and also enjoying a day out. I'm trying to think about something else, but I can't help noticing that it makes him look rather windswept and interesting (if you're into that sort of thing, of course).

'Are you listening to a word I'm saying?' he asks. 'There's a pop quiz afterwards, I should warn you.' He grins a gigantic grin like he's the funniest boy alive while I stare at his white teeth that aren't quite straight. His bright smile measures somewhere between perfect and interesting. Not that I'm into that sort of thing, of course.

'I'm listening,' I reply and nod my head slowly.

'Come on, this is our stop.' Sam pulls himself towards the front of the bus using the seat backrests for support. I follow his lead and step down onto a tar road that's hot and hectic. With a day full of stops to make, the bus soon chugs off again, leaving us faced with a foreground of colourful stripes rippling in the sun. The black ribbon of road gives way to the brown streak of boardwalk that ends in a broad band of scratched blue water that disappears into a smooth turquoise sky. The pebbled beach is steep and dips anonymously between the brown and blue stripes.

'Cross with me,' Sam orders and grabs my hand. I don't really have a choice because he's got me hooked up and towed across the road before I can even attempt to protest the fact that I have crossed a road before.

The boardwalk is busy with naked torsos and sunhats and the air rattles with the sounds of crashing surf and snappy seagulls. Sam is still holding my hand. 'Ahem?' I cough and aim eyeballs at his fingers locked around mine.

'Oh right, sorry,' he smiles sheepishly and releases me. 'The important thing is that we made it across the road safely.'

I nod solemnly. He's very considerate; he makes a nice boy friend (spot the difference). 'So where to first?'

'How about we take a walk up to Brighton Pier?' he suggests. 'There's loads to see.'

'Sounds good.' And we set off side by side, neither of us in a hurry and both at ease in each other's company.

Sam points out the attractions he thinks I'll find intriguing, like the bones of the West Pier and the multi-coloured Marina in the distance. He even knows about something called Regency architecture which is apparently studded along the seafront. I don't say much and just enjoy the fact that I really don't have to. I feel awkward around most people and usually worry about making the sort of conversation they'll find interesting, but with Sam I don't even give it a moment's thought. I don't even have to think about being something that I'm not.

Suddenly we're faced with a tall sheet of grey metal jutting out of the boardwalk. It's almost three times my height and about a metre in width and covered in what looks like engravings of various people kissing. There's a father kissing a baby, an old couple…I count about twelve people in total. Twelve people all smooching. Right.

'So what's this then?' I ask.

Sam grins and winks. 'That's the Kissing Wall.'

'You're kidding.'

'No way, that's what it is: the Kissing Wall.'

'What's it for?' I ask – and then instantly wish I hadn't.

'It brings good luck and eternal love to those who

lock lips in front of it.' He's still grinning at me.

'You're having me on, right?'

'Nope. Oh OK, yes I am,' he surrenders. 'It is called the Kissing Wall but it's meant to be a work of art, that's all.'

I stare at him blankly for a few moments; I haven't met a Sam before. 'Good try,' I commend him with a *you-didn't-fool-me* smile and nod of the head.

'My favourite part of the seafront is coming up.' He points to the bleached shop fronts ahead. 'That's the Artist's Quarter, you'll love it!' He steps up his pace and I follow in his wake, egged on by his infectious energy.

The Artist's Quarter is a spread of sea-facing shops selling floor-to-ceiling paintings, sculptures and displays of exotic, quirky artworks you'd need more than a week to suck up. Artists' pampered creations and captivating knick-knacks spill out of shop openings and onto the walkway – some clambering up walls and doors and others languishing on the baking pavements, all eager to show themselves off in the silver light that's bouncing off the ocean. Random terracotta pots, bursting with burnt-orange flowers, also reach for the limelight, determined to make an impression and net some of the passing interest, while faded lifebuoys, rope art and striking bits of curled up driftwood crowd into the corners – adding to the seaside ambience without even trying. There's magic everywhere.

'Oi Sam!' A voice calls out to our left. A bald man with a stained apron sitting on a deckchair beneath a washed out canvas umbrella is watching us expectantly. He has a pair of half-moon reading glasses perched on the tip of his nose.

'Hey Archie,' Sam waves as he approaches the man.

'How are you, wee laddie?' Archie asks in a Scots accent that's so thick it sounds gooey. The bare legs sticking out of his apron and basking in the sun are covered in a web of blue cheese veins.

'Fine thanks, Arch. This is my friend, Libby.'

I step forward and show my palm in greeting. 'Hi there.'

'Well hellooo Libby,' Archie sings enthusiastically.

'Er, hi,' I say again.

His smile swaps from my face to Sam's. 'I sold one for you.'

'That's great!' Sam cheers.

'Here you go, fella.' Archie offers Sam a note from the pouch of his apron.

My friend grins and slips the money into a pocket. 'Thanks very much.'

'Got a lady customer interested in this here one,'

Archie adds, pointing to a small square mirror framed in a mosaic of shells, driftwood and beach pebbles. 'She said she'd be by later this afternoon.'

'Cool, let's hope so,' Sam replies. 'And thanks again, Arch.'

'Now don't you be mentioning it,' the older man waves him off. 'And you have yourselves a glorious afternoon.'

'Will do,' Sam salutes. 'Ciao for now.'

'Toodle-loo,' Archie chimes.

'Er, bye then,' I blither, raise my palm for the second time and follow after Sam. 'So what was that about?'

'I make those mirrors,' he explains, 'and Archie sells them for me.'

'Wow! They're really pretty.' I wonder what Sophie would make of Sam. She'd probably poke fun at his juggling act and homemade mirrors. She'd definitely say that he was geeky, which only makes me like him even more. Sam does what makes Sam happy – he's true to himself and I admire his courage.

'I've got something planned especially for you,' he reveals suddenly.

'And what's that?' I can't keep the suspicion from my voice; I don't trust surprises.

'The Ghost Train,' he growls and crumples his face.

He obviously thinks he looks menacing. 'You like funfairs, don't you?'

'Sure, but what makes you think I'm a big fan of the Ghost Train?'

'I saw your book...*Reincarnation for Believers*, so I figured you must have a ghoulish side. And it's my treat.' He extracts the still-warm note Archie handed him just a short while ago.

Reincarnation for Believers? Ah yes, I completely forgot that I'll be dying one day soon, which is a bit of a bummer really because I haven't felt this happy in ages. We're having such a great day, how do I begin to explain to Sam that *Reincarnation for Believers* is a bit more than simply a sideline interest? I guess I don't. I just try and look forward to the Ghost Train instead.

'Let's get moving,' Sam suggests, oblivious to my inner turmoil, 'we may have to queue.'

I nod and we head straight for the illuminated red and yellow Brighton Pier sign up ahead, but we don't bother hanging about – Sam is only interested in the Ghost Train ride right at the very end of the pier. I'm not quite as fixated and take the opportunity to gaze out over the glossy lace-metal railings to the tetchy waves and shrinking seafront behind us. I have to side-step a group of tourists tossing greasy fried chips to the seagulls and

I almost run into a jaywalking family, slurping on soggy cones of thawing ice-cream, but we finally make it to the end of the pier where pop music is belting out across the scuffed wooden decking.

The painted ghouls and goblins of the Ghost Train stand out against the churning sky, promising to bring doom, danger and dread to all those who dare to enter. We don't have to queue for very long and before I know it, we're strapped into a two-seater fibreglass cart that's shaped like a bat with its wings wrapped around us. A life-size skeleton with glowing eyes waves us on, laughing manically as it does so.

'Why are skeletons so calm?' Sam leans over and whispers in my ear.

'I have no idea.'

'Because nothing gets under their skin!' He thinks he's side-splitting.

The giant bat gives a shake and a shudder and then lurches forward on its tracks towards a steep, ascending, spiral ramp. We're not quite halfway to the top when the bat's motors start crying and screaming out in agony. Sam and I glance at each other and then down at the retreating pier below. Our knuckles gripping the locking bar are as hard and sharp as bones. So we're terrified – but not of *ghosts*! But we eventually grind our way painfully to the top of the ramp and slide into the murky mouth of the Ghost Train tunnel. Now we're travelling along a gloomy corridor pitted with monster-filled alcoves, dangling cobwebs and cackling creatures. Grrr, my talking thoughts give a dull roar. The bat on wheels begins chugging down towards what looks like a solid brick wall. We're gathering momentum and just when it looks like we're about to become one with the bricks the train tracks do a sharp U-turn, taking our bat along with it. So that was a narrow escape then. Yawn. I'm as cool as a February morning. Not even the life-size model of a man squirming on an electric chair ruffles me. What does finally get me is a very bright light that flashes in my face and a piercing whistle that screeches simultaneously in my ear. Suddenly I'm less cool. I shriek, jump in the air, land and grab the nearest hand in one rapid movement. The hand is Sam's.

'Er, sorry,' I stutter and feel the burn on my cheeks.

'No problem.' He smiles his white teeth but doesn't fight for his hand.

A Dracula voice appears to tell us to count our friends as we leave, and then we're discharged out into the bright light. I would remove my hand but Sam is grinning at me like he doesn't have a single care in the entire world, and I suddenly want to feel that way too. There's something different about Sam; I feel lighter when I'm with him, like the weight of the world is no longer strapped to my back. And this is probably why I don't undo our fingers. It's the only reason I can think of, anyway.

So, still holding hands, we leave the bat and start walking, but this time we don't choose a destination and we're less interested in the scenery. We're just two people out walking. Sam just has to ask about my family and I blab almost everything. I tell him how I miss my mum and that I'm lost without her; I explain that spending my life saying goodbye to her is making me sick inside; I describe how my father isn't necessarily a bad guy but we're like two strangers who will never understand one another; I insist that a girl definitely needs her mum; and finally – I bare all and admit that I just don't belong anywhere any more.

Insignificant things like seconds and minutes dissolve into nothing and by the time we sit down near a fountain amongst the vibrant greenery called Steine Gardens to munch on the sandwiches we bought from a vendor I've told Sam just about everything, everything except that I'm frightened and absolutely certain that I'm going to die one day very soon. But I'm not used to opening up – I usually squash everything deep down inside me, and I'm now starting to find the drone of my voice just a little unsettling.

'When I think about the terrible things that some people go through,' I begin my conclusion, 'I know that I don't have it all that bad. But I guess you just can't help the way you feel, can you?'

Sam sighs and squeezes my hand. We still haven't let go. 'To belong is an important basic human need,' he begins. 'You shouldn't underestimate that. Everyone needs a place to lay down their roots. That way you can stand tall and strong when life tries to knock you over. A family and a home give you the grounding and confidence to know who you are; it saves you from blowing about like tumbleweed. You're still trying to adjust to the changes, but you'll find your place in time, Libs.'

'So what makes you the expert?' I laugh dryly, suddenly feeling awkward. 'You're one of the most confident and grounded people I've ever met. I wish I could be like you.'

'I have to work at my confidence too. But you can't leave your happiness to chance.'

'What does that mean?'

'It means that you have to take charge of it. These are

the cards you've been dealt, nothing will change that and regret is a waste of energy. But do you think you can try and search for the positives and make them work to your advantage?'

'I appreciate your advice Sam,' I exhale softly, 'but you don't know what it's like. Saying goodbye is the toughest thing in the world.'

Sam doesn't say anything; he just smiles and gives my hand another reassuring squeeze, like he'll keep on trying until he finally does understand. This means a lot to me and without planning to, I settle on number seven of My Dying To Do List: I think I should kiss a boy. Or more specifically – I should definitely kiss Sam one day before I die.

fifteen
it might seem mean

I'm trying to concentrate on my remembrance collage for Tommy but all I keep thinking about is Sam. I've just realised that I spent all day yesterday talking about me, I and myself without asking him a single question about himself. He must think I'm seriously self-centred; I'll have to make sure that next time I'm the one asking all the questions.

Sam made loads of sense yesterday and I've been giving his advice a lot of thought. He's right – it's time I took charge of my happiness. Things are only impossible until they're not. And I can't leave it to chance any longer. Regardless of Mum's promises for the future, if I want to move to Brighton to be with her then I'm the one who's got to make it possible. And something is telling me that when I do, the natural balance and order of things might be restored and who knows, maybe then I won't have to die any more. There's a chance that once everything is back to how it should be my destiny will take another path and I won't be doomed any longer.

There's only one thing – or person – standing in the way of my move to be with my mum, and his name is Mick. And although I'm sure he's a nice enough guy and all blah-blah of that, the plain fact of the matter is that he's coming between my mum and me. And I've got to be tough; this is no time for soft sentimentality. He's planted daft ideas in her head about them living together and starting a brand new life, but what he doesn't realise is that I appreciate my mum too, and she's the only one who appreciates me. And two's company three's a crowd, it's that simple. So watch out Chicken Mick, Liberty Belle is about to do kung-fu for her happiness!

Right now I'm alternating between staring out of the living-room window and painting a small picture of waves crashing on the beach below the postcard of Gustav Klimt's *Mother and Child*. I thought Tommy might like to know how much I loved the ocean, which is why I've borrowed Mum's watercolours and I'm carefully applying them to the remembrance collage. I'm not very artistic and the fishing boat bobbing along the waves looks more like half an avocado, but right now I'm too busy thinking about other things to really care. I still have no idea how I'm going to put Mum off Mick, but something will come to mind. I just have to be patient and give it plenty of thought.

I can hear the phone ringing but I don't take much notice of it either – it's only when the shrill sound is replaced by Lotus hollering for me to take a call that I finally look up and abandon the view from the window for the phone in the kitchen.

'Your father wants to speak with you,' Lotus mouths silently and waves the outstretched receiver in the air.

My father never calls me at Mum's; what have or haven't I done now? 'Hello?'

'Hello Libby, this is your father.'

That's the rumour, the thoughts quip. 'Hi.'

'Hello. Uh…so, are you having a good time with Your Mother in Brighton then?' My father has one telephone voice which he uses for both business and personal calls.

'Yes thanks.'

'What have you been doing?'

It's not like my father to show interest in my trips to Brighton and I absorb his curiosity for a few silent moments. I can hear a baby crying and scratchy grandparent voices nattering loudly in the background. That must be Tommy with Misty's parents then.

'Not much,' I finally reply.

'Oh, right.'

Silence.

'How is Tomm...er, Thomas getting on?' I ask.

'He's doing great – a real little champ. Listen Liberty, I'm sorry we argued about his christening.'

He doesn't add anything further and I try to digest his apology. I appreciate the effort, but nothing can ever change the fact that I missed the big event and that's all that really matters to me now. My brother's christening is a day I can never have back again. My parents might find it easy to pick and choose between their loved ones, but I don't think it's fair that I was made to pick between my brother and my mother.

'It's fine,' I say instead. The female older voice in the background has grown louder and I can hear her saying something about finding Nemo.

'Marion please, do you mind...' my father hisses. Marion doesn't reply. 'Sorry Liberty,' my father's voice reappears.

'It's fine,' I repeat.

Neither of us speaks for a few seconds. 'So Thomas really likes Pippen,' he finally says, only this time his voice is slightly hushed.

So you know I overheard you guys arguing then, my talking thoughts dig, and now you're trying to be nice to me but you don't want the Misty mob to hear you talking about Mum's old friend Pippen. I've never really thought about it before, but my father's life may just be more complicated than my own.

'That's good,' I respond simply.

'So, shall I call you again in a few days' time?'

'Sure, if you like.' That's never happened before either.

'Well, goodbye then,' he says.

'Bye-bye.' I put the phone down and stare at Lotus, who is hovering within eavesdropping distance.

'So how's your father?' she asks.

'He's fine I guess.' Why is everyone suddenly so interested in everyone else?

Quick to take a hint, Lotus swiftly changes the subject. 'So how do you fancy hanging out with me tonight?'

'Why, where's my mum going?'

'Oh, I'd forget my own third eye if it wasn't in the middle of my forehead!' she cackles. 'Mick called a short while ago – he's surprising your mum and taking her out for a romantic meal to her favourite restaurant, *Green Leaves*.' The look on my face obviously says it all. 'He did ask if you would mind, Libby, and well – it *is* the anniversary of the day they met so I assured him you would be happy to spend an evening with me. You are, aren't you?'

''Course,' I huff.

'Hey, we'll have a brill time together,' she grins and rubs my head while I stand there wishing she wouldn't. I hate people touching my head.

'I've got to finish my painting before Mum gets home from the Kooky Centre,' I brood and return to the remembrance collage still waiting for me in front of the living-room window.

sixteen
creating a scene

Lotus has simply told Mum to dress pretty and be ready by eight, and Mum has complied. I'm in the bathroom when I hear her calling for me. I also do as I'm told.

Mick is standing in the minimalist living room dressed in long navy trousers, an open-neck collar shirt and slip-on sandals that are more biblical and less Roman than the pair with lace-up leather ankle thongs. His hair is still damp and combed back from his face in sweeping grooves, and he smells strong and sweet.

'Look who's here!' Mum grins at me exuberantly like she just won Blind Date. She's dressed in a pale pink sari skirt with gold brocade that matches the swirling patterns on her pale pink top. She's also wearing open sandals, only this time her toes are painted with silver and purple stars. New Agers have a thing about their feet, my talking thoughts observe dryly.

'Hiya Mick,' I grin cheerily. He nods, smiles and gives me a small wave but doesn't say anything. Now he's rocking nervously on the soles of his sandalled feet and looking seasick.

'Mick has booked us a special table at *Green Leaves*,' Mum gushes. Her eyes are wide and her smile is stretched to forever.

'Well, that's wonderful!' I gush back.

'We won't be late,' Mick updates Lotus and then turns to Mum. 'Shall we get going then?'

'Yes, of course,' she twitters.

'Great, I'll just grab my bag,' I declare and dash in the direction of the dining room where my embroidered shoulder bag is ready and waiting on the futon. So it's not brilliant; it's the only plan I could come up with. I'm only gone a few seconds and when I return everyone is exactly as I left them, except their sandals are now sharing floor space with their jaws.

'Uh…' Mum is the first to retrieve hers.

'Sorry about that.' I grin like it's Christmas morning. 'Boy am I starving!' I don't give anyone time to protest and hurriedly scoot out of the front door with a farewell wave to Lotus. I'm already waiting at the car by the time Mick and Mum eventually follow, the first looking confused and the other wearing a frown. I think I might have overheard Mum apologising, but it's a windy night so she really could've been saying anything.

Nobody says a word during the drive to the restaurant and eventually Mick pops an old battered tape into the cassette player mounted on the car's crusty dashboard. Mick's wheels are even older than Aurora. The fake-leather backseat I'm sitting on has perished in places and I pick nervously at its cracked, tattered edges while I try to ignore the tension buzzing in the air. I must try and listen to the crooning cowboy welcoming me to a hotel in California via the car speakers instead. Still, I'm finding it difficult to relax and by the time we reach *Green Leaves* I'm beginning to wonder if this was such a good idea after all. But it's way too late to turn back now. And besides, I knew that beating Mick to my mum wasn't necessarily going to be easy. I've just got to stick to the plan.

We enter the restaurant where a man with dark, oiled-back hair dressed in a sharp white suit is waiting to greet us.

'Your name please, sir?' he asks with a polished flourish.

'The table is under Edwards,' Mick mumbles.

'Right you are,' Oil Slick sings seamlessly. 'That's a table for uh…two then?' His head slides up and down while he mentally counts each one of us.

'We're three now,' Mick says apologetically.

'Mmm.' Our host contemplates a large book in front of him and elegantly taps his manicured forefinger against his front teeth. 'You did request a cosy table by the window, sir, and I'm afraid we are fully booked. It might be a bit of a squeeze, but the best we can do is to add another chair to your table for you.'

'That'll be fine,' Mick nods and shoves his hands deep inside his navy pockets.

I look away and focus my attention on the NO SMOKING signs stuck everywhere. Very sensible. Having a smoking section in a restaurant is a bit like having a peeing section in a swimming pool. I'm being careful to keep my eyes pointed away from Mum and I zone in on the bustling room behind her instead. But I can still feel the heat of her glower warming my left side. I also catch her toes doing star jumps as her right foot tap-tap-taps on the tiled floor in irritation. She's very unimpressed with me right now; I'm obviously ruining their evening completely. A sudden spurt of guilt gushes over me but I quickly plug it with some basic reasoning – courtesy of my talking thoughts. I'm not a leper, so why should my company ruin their evening in the first place? And it's not like I'm around 24/7 either, which means that they can have their stupid romantic dinners any old time. If anyone is cutting in, it's definitely Mick. And besides, my mother and I share DNA – I doubt Mick can top that. So if anyone is the outsider, once again it's definitely Chicken Mick. Guilt be gone!

Oil Slick was not kidding when he said that the table near the window was cosy – it's about the size of a manhole cover. It would have been a squeeze for the two of them anyway, so what's one more. All three chairs have a view of the ocean and I claim the middle seat. I'm in for it anyway – I may as well jump with both feet. Mick squeezes past a large leafy palm and presses himself into the chair to my left, while Mum slumps down into the chair to my right. Our foreheads are practically touching and I'm grateful that there isn't a candle on the table. That might be dangerous, for so many reasons.

'Shall I order some wine then?' Mick finally begins the conversation. And even though I know that he's talking to Mum, I'm settling into my new role as meddling minx.

'Oh, no thanks Mick,' I beam cheerily, 'Mum and I believe that alcohol is a slippery downhill slope. But you go ahead, if you feel you need it to enjoy yourself.' Mum really can't pull me up on that one; she gave me the *you-don't-need-alcohol-to-have-a-good-time* speech not so long ago.

'No no, what was I thinking?' Mick sighs sadly. 'Mineral water all round then?'

'There are enough people in the world dying of

poverty, hunger and thirst,' I smile kindly, 'I'm happy with tap water, thank you.'

'Right, so that's three tap waters then,' Mick informs our waiter, whose eyeballs stretch to the ceiling. Another cheapskate, he grieves for his tip.

'Thank you, Mick.' This is the first time Mum has spoken and her face is open and apologetic. My talking thoughts tell me she wasn't saying thank you for the tap water.

'So my father called this morning.' I turn to Mum. And why wouldn't I tell her about the phone call, it's the truth. 'He asked if I was having a good time. And he asked how you were.' OK, so that's not entirely true, but I'm only saying this because I really want my parents to start being nicer to each another. So it's one of the reasons anyway.

'He's probably missing you.' Mum smiles through clenched teeth and narrows her eyes at me.

I pretend I don't notice and blither along merrily. 'Anyway, so I told him you're very well and that you love living with Lotus and you're going to buy me an open annual train ticket so that I can visit as often as I like which means it'll almost be like three girls living in a cottage on the beach.'

'That's ni—' Mum begins.

'You know, I think he regrets certain things,' I push forward. 'I don't mean the divorce necessarily, but I don't suppose you can have twelve years together and then just develop amnesia overnight.'

The waiter arrives with our tap water and Mum unhooks her clenched jaw to take a long sip of hers.

'Can you?' I ask. But I don't wait for her answer. 'Yes, I'd say twelve years is rather a long time to share someone's life.' I don't think Mum has realised that I'm no longer talking about my father and she quite obviously wants me to change the subject.

'That's enough, Libby,' she orders quietly.

'Do you have any children, Mick?' I turn away from Mum and ask in a jovial getting-to-know-you sort of way.

'Uh, no I don't,' he replies. He looks like someone with a bull's-eye drawn on their face.

'Oh right, you just never really felt the need to settle down and start a family then?' I keep my words soft and sweet, just in case I have to eat them later.

'Liberty!' Mum snaps.

'Not everyone is into commitment, I understand that,' I nod sagely and take a deep drink of my water. I'm not really enjoying this game any more, but I have no idea how to reverse out of the cramped corner I've meddled my way in to. Desperate for something to do I open the menu and concentrate on choosing something to eat. My options include tofu and seaweed pasties, apple and sage sausages, rice-stuffed aubergine and hazelnut roast. Now I understand why the restaurant is called *Green Leaves*. I should have known the food would be vegetarian.

'What are you going to have, Mick?' Mum leans forward in her chair and asks tenderly. I have to bend backwards to avoid being head-butted.

'I think I'll have the tried-and-tested mushroom bake.'

'And I'll have the sausages,' I say. 'So what are you having, Mum?'

'I think I'll have the same as Mick,' she replies and gives him a warm smile.

'And I think I'll have some of these nibbles – I'm ravenous!' I announce and dunk my hand into the bowl of trail-mix looking snacks in the middle of the table. I suppose plain old bread isn't good enough for these New Age types, they must have their daily dose of seeds and nuts.

'Errrggh!' I suddenly projectile-spit the trail mix out of my mouth and into my half full glass of water. These nibbles taste absolutely disgusting – like crunchy deodorant.

Suddenly Mum and Mick are giggling. Now they're laughing loud enough to turn heads. They're starting to embarrass me.

'What's so funny?' I squirm. 'I don't know how you can eat that stuff, it tastes revolting!'

'We don't eat *that stuff*,' Mum hiccups, 'because it's pot-pourri. You're just meant to smell it.'

'If you're that hungry maybe you should order a starter instead of eating the décor,' Mick joins in, clucking hysterically. My gaffe has broken the ice as well as my ego. They're having a jolly old time while I'm staring at my water glass and watching the half chewed pot-pourri drifting slowly to the bottom. Life is a joke and I think I'm the punchline. What sort of restaurant puts pot-pourri in the middle of the table anyway, my talking thoughts seethe. A daft New Age restaurant, that's what! And I'll tell you one more thing, this Mick even laughs like a chicken.

I don't say very much else for the rest of the evening and even though the three of us are practically touching noses, after a while I think Mum and Mick almost forget that I'm there. Of course I make one or two half-hearted final attempts to assert myself in front of this man who likes to sneak my mum special knowing winks, but my fire is out and I really just want to get out of this place. I also want to brush my teeth; five glasses of tap water later and I still have the taste of pot-pourri in my mouth.

Mum has spent the last few days working at the Kooky Centre while I've spent most of my time with Sam either visiting the beach, helping him with his mirrors, or just generally larking about. Mum keeps trying to corner me with the words, 'we need to talk', but so far I've managed to duck and dive out of any stern heart-to-hearts she has planned. Still, I doubt I can hold her off for much longer.

Today I'm at Sam's house helping him and his mum make banners, masks and signboards for a protest march they have planned for the streets of Brighton in one week's time. Gloria is a member of the *End War Now* lobby, which – as I understand it – basically protests against war in general. I've never been a part of a protest march before (my father would rupture a vital organ if he knew), and so far I'm having a blast (the non-violent kind, it goes without saying).

Of course I agree with the basic principles of *End War Now* (like who needs it!), but what I'm really enjoying is being a part of this group of people who all appear to be so tightly bound by their common interests, belief systems and goals. There really is strength in numbers, especially when you belong. Various members of *End War Now* have been trailing in and out of Sam and Gloria's house throughout the day offering exuberant greetings, heartfelt backslaps and dispersing enthusiastic words of encouragement to one another. They're like one big happy family. I can't help noticing how they all seem to appreciate one another and the efforts they're making towards the common cause, and I'm still glowing from the passionate praise my BUILD TRUST NOT BOMBS banner has received. It seems I may even 'have a talent for this sort of thing'.

By mid-afternoon the number of visitors has dwindled but that's OK, because we've done enough work and bonding for one day. I left home this morning dressed in jeans and a black T-shirt printed with the simple phrase GET OVER IT. Now I'm wearing barefaced pride and a white *End War Now* campaign shirt that's two sizes too big. Just then Gloria's face appears around the door.

'I'm off to run a few errands,' she announces, 'I'll be back in a bit.'

Sam waves, I smile and Gloria disappears.

'I reckon we've done our bit for the day,' Sam

announces, stretching his cramped spine, 'how about some flower sticks one-on-one?'

'I didn't bring my flower sticks,' I reply truthfully. Plus I'm not in the mood, my talking thoughts moan.

'You can use mine.'

'Oh. Thanks.' Sam disappears upstairs and returns with the flower sticks as promised, then heads outdoors for some fresh air. I reluctantly follow.

'Right, now let's see how far you've progressed with these babies,' he begins, handing me his flower sticks.

How do I tell Sam that I haven't progressed even a tiny bit? 'How about you give me a quick refresher course first?' I suggest. That's one way.

'You haven't been practising, have you?' He scolds me with a wink and a playful growl. 'Right, now first you put this stick in this hand and that stick in that hand.' I accept the sticks from Sam as instructed and stand there stupidly. I can't even remember how to begin.

'What are you like!' he tut-tuts and manoeuvres himself directly behind me so that his front is pressing against my back and his forearms are parallel to my own. He then covers my hands gently with his own and delivers instructions directly into my ear. 'The first thing you need to concentrate on is your rhythm,' he begins. 'You want to create a see-saw motion. See…one, two, one, two.' He's moving my hands with their sticks in time to his voice and although I'm trying really hard to apply myself and learn the lesson, having Sam's warm body pressed up against my own is quickly proving to be rather unsettling. My hands are like jelly and so is my brain. His clean, spicy smell is overwhelming my senses and tripping up my thought processes; I couldn't concentrate on these flower sticks if my life depended on it.

'You need to keep your hands firm and strong so that you can support and bounce the tasselled stick,' Sam continues, still oblivious to the fact that I am now in idiot mode. His breath is hot against my ear and fanning my hair so that it tickles my cheek. 'Are you even listening?' he clucks patiently. His lips scrape briefly against my ear and a million goose bumps detonate like landmines along the length of my arms.

'Uh, I think I might be a bit tired for the flower sticks today,' I gulp and take a few quick safe steps away from him while rubbing my palms along my arms, hoping to flatten the bumps before he notices anything.

'Are you cold?' he asks.

'Nope, in fact it's nice to be outside for a change.' I plop down on the grass and stretch my legs out in front of me.

Sam drops down next to me and starts fooling about with the sticks like a pro. 'So what's up?' he asks.

'I told you I had the co-ords of a wombat,' I apologise.

'Forget about the flower sticks, I mean what's up with you? You seem preoccupied.'

I can't very well tell Sam about *Green Leaves* or Mick, he'll think I'm a raging cow for sure. 'Everything is fine. Tell me a bit about your family, like where does your father live?' I ask instead.

'Why do you want to know about my father all of a sudden?' Sam laughs.

'I don't know. I guess we spent the other day talking all about me; I don't know very much about you at all.'

'There's not much to tell. But in answer to your question, no my father is not around. I haven't seen him for a very long time.'

Sam doesn't offer up any further information and I'm reluctant to push for more. Conversations about AWOL parents are far too delicate to be forced. Sam repositions himself and settles back into the grass with his face to the clouds, and while he's wiggling about to get comfy his right foot comes to rest beside mine. Our naked toes are touching – barely, but there's contact. I don't know if he's done this intentionally or if he's even noticed, but I'm too jumpy to risk an enquiring peek. And besides,

I'm enjoying the closeness of this boy who I've already decided to kiss soon – before I die – and so I leave my foot exactly where it is.

'How much do you know about Mick then?' I ask, trying to sound as nonchalant as possible.

'Mick?' Sam repeats. 'Mmm...not very much, except that he's always just sort of been around. He's a quiet guy but nice enough, I reckon. How do you feel about him dating your mum?'

I want to explain to Sam that it's not really Mick I have anything personal against (although I do think the denim hot pants issue needs to be addressed); it's the space he's taking up in my mum's life that I have a problem with. And I have a problem with it because that's space with my name on it. It's bad enough Mum and I don't live together any more, but since Mick arrived on the scene she seems distracted, like her head is somewhere else. She's had enough time to settle down in Brighton. The way I see it, he's sidetracked her attention away from the fact that she and I belong with one another.

'I can't be arsed about Mick either way,' I finally speak out loud. I wouldn't normally say things like that, but I'm suddenly feeling exposed and the only way I know how to cover this up is to sound hard and heavy, even though I know it doesn't really suit me. When in doubt, make it sound convincing. Sam doesn't say anything but I can feel him watching me out of the corner of his eye. 'I've taken your advice by the way,' I continue, subtly swinging the subject in another direction. 'I'm finally taking charge of my own happiness. I'm not leaving it in the clumsy hands of fate any more.'

'Oh good,' Sam smiles and rolls onto his side so that he's buttressed by his elbow. 'And what exactly are you doing?'

Well this is how it is, I start rehearsing my speech. For the past few months I've been convinced that I'm going to die one day soon. I'm not sure exactly when or how; I've simply known that it's going to happen in the near future. The feeling is usually strongest when I'm lying in bed at night alone in the dark and thinking about my life and things like saying goodbye to my mum. Anyway, now that my father and Misty and Tommy are their own family I was going to ask Mum if I could come and live with her for a bit. But before I could pop the question she told me all about Mick and how she likes him so much they're planning on moving in together soon. So I didn't ask her. I was too scared she'd say no because she has plans with Mick. Then you said that I should take control of my own happiness. So I figured there's only one thing to do: and that's to get Mum to dump Mick so that I can move to Brighton. Because that means you and I can be together too, Sam. Double-whammy bonus, because you really are the only true friend I have (Sophie's friendship comes with too much small print). And I figured that if I was back with my mum again it might restore the balance and natural order of things and maybe when my life is on an even keel I won't have to die any more. Mum is always going on about Gaia the Earth Goddess and maintaining the balance of the universe so who knows, it's worth a try because I don't know that I'm really ready to die just yet. So that's my plan – that's how I'm taking charge of my own happiness. What do you think? My talking thoughts blurt it all out in my head but the words don't make it into the open air.

'Libby?' Sam asks.

'Uh huh?'

'I'm still waiting for you to tell me how you're taking charge of your happiness.'

'Yes, I will…one day,' I reply, staring down at the tips of our naked toes that are still touching.

eighteen
the cat with the cream

I've been waiting outside the Kooky Centre for Mum for fifteen minutes already and I'm starting to lose all feeling in my legs, which are wearing shorts – even though it's as cold as Christmas. Today began foggy but I predicted it would burn away to reveal warm blue skies. I was *very* wrong. The sun has pulled a sickie and today is gloomy and cold, just like me. Mum and Lotus have gone to donate blood and Sam is standing in for Archie at the Artist's Quarter so I've spent the afternoon searching second-hand bookshops for a copy of *The Happy Prince* by Oscar Wilde, which was my favourite story when I was a kid. I'd like Tommy to have a copy, just in case I'm not around to take him to the library. I didn't find one.

I glance at my wristwatch for the hundredth time and hop about like a beginner ballerina with my shoulders bunched around my ears. Mum is now twenty minutes late. Just then my brand new mobile phone beeps with a text message. I press the green button. It's Mum, and she's telling me to go and have a drink inside the Kooky

Centre – she won't be much longer. OK, so she just called it *the Centre*.

The bamboo sign above the double doors reads Centre for Sumskiri Khuki in bold painted letters; I've never been inside the Kooky Centre before. I push one of the heavy doors open and the tarred pavement gives way to a dark concrete floor that's studded with smooth, round pebbles like the ones on the beach. The air smells of multivitamins and sounds like a rainforest. I can hear birds singing and water rushing, but I can't see either. I think Mum has this CD at home.

It takes a few moments for my eyes to adjust to the soft lighting; according to the small pointed signboards mounted on the rattan room dividers I have choices. I can either continue straight ahead to the Elixir Juice Bar, the Enchanted Spirit Bookstore and the Mystic Unicorn Gift Shop, or I can turn a sharp left and commit to Fifth Dimension Movement. I keep walking straight. I'm going to do as I'm told and find something to drink. I'm already in enough hoo-ha with my mother as it is.

According to the signs, to get to the Elixir Juice Bar I must follow a sweep of silver metal steps, and when I reach the top I find myself facing a pool of chairs with tables overlooking the Centre. The place is almost empty except for a tall woman with long dark hair sitting at a table with her head stuck in a newspaper, and a young man with a goatee beard and a green and red knitted cap working behind the juice-bar counter. I approach slowly; this is the Kooky Centre, after all. The young man eyeballs my approach but doesn't say anything. As I get closer I notice two things: he's dicing celery on a chopping board, and his goatee beard is plaited with green and red beads. I can feel myself staring, so I tilt my head up and run my eyes along the board behind Billy Goat's head instead. Mega-Veggie Shake…Wheatgrass Shot…Green Gaia Smoothie… Zen Tea. I don't see Coca-Cola anywhere.

'I'll have the Organic Pineapple Blast,' I order dejectedly. That should make me one with the universe.

'In or out?' he asks.

'Of what?' I mumble.

'Will you be having that here or are you taking it away with you?' He says this slowly, like I'm not very bright or foreign or something.

Why didn't you just say that in the first place, my talking thoughts gripe. I don't usually like to encourage them, but today they have a point. 'In,' I huff and head for a stool at the other end of the counter.

Billy sets to work on my Pineapple Blast and I sit and

try not to stare. I hadn't noticed until now, but the bar is piped with soothing electronic music that sounds seriously space age, like there's a chilled-out Martian DJ lounging just behind the glass mirror. Billy appears and sets a tall glass of yellow fizzing juice down in front of me. With a flourish he then produces a plastic bottle with a nozzle and squeezes a jet of dark green liquid into the drink. I really wish he hadn't done that.

'Bottoms up,' he barks and I almost jump to my feet. Ah right, not my bottom. Billy is staring at me expectantly and making me edgy. I hesitantly lift the glass and take a micro-sip of the muddy drink. Satisfied, he finally returns to his chopping board and the celery. Ugh! Organic Pineapple Blast tastes like raw spinach.

Just then a short man dressed in a black suit with a matching felt hat enters the bar and heads straight over to the tall woman reading the newspaper just a few metres to my right. She hears him approach and looks up from her paper. Mum says everyone is beautiful in their own way, but I can't help wondering if she meant this woman too. With her thick skin and large, heavy features she's not what you'd call conventionally pretty, and her gaudy make-up has a blotchy, paint-by-numbers look about it too – emphasising rather than enhancing her looks. Her long dark hair is nice enough though, perhaps there lies her beauty.

'Are you ready, poppet?' the petite man asks her. I feel a little sorry for this bloke too, it can't be easy being so delicate. The woman nods and stands up to her full height, showing off her long satin evening dress. *Hello Kooky Centre!*

'Sure am,' replies the woman, who sounds just like Mick.

MICK!?!

I slouch behind my Pineapple Blast and peer out at the woman who just so happens to sound like my mum's boyfriend. It can happen; people can sound alike – even men and women. What a coincidence. I stare hard past her make-up and long brown hair. And that's when I realise – with gut-twisting certainty – that it *is* actually Mick, aka my dear mum's weirdo boyfriend who, it turns out, just so happens to enjoy dressing up in ladies evening wear when she's not around! I flip my eyes over to the man in the suit one last time – just to be sure, even though I've already grasped what's going on here. The man in the black suit and felt hat is really a woman. What kind of sicko sex-swapping arrangement is this!

The man-who-is-really-a-woman reaches for the woman-who-is-really-a-man who is actually Chicken

Mick and takes her hand (or his hand, depending on how you're looking at it). I turn to give Billy an incredulous *what the heck is going on here* gawp but he's too busy blending something. Mick staggers past me toward the silver stairs, his patent leather high heels clip-clopping on the tiled floor. He's concentrating on keeping up with the woman in the suit and still hasn't noticed me or my protruding eyeballs.

'See you two at the *Aquarius*!' Billy suddenly shouts out after the cross-dressing couple.

Ah, so he's in on it then! My talking thoughts catch on quick. Neither of them shouts a reply back, although Mick does give a joyful side-kick of his right heel just before disappearing around the corner. The sight of it just about tips me over the edge of my stool. I grab a hold of the counter and stare at the newspaper deserted on the table, and that's when everything swiftly turns clear and bright. This really isn't such tragic news after all. When Mum finds out that Mick is way *too* in touch with his feminine side she'll dump him for sure, which means that I can come and live in Brighton with her and see Sam. And I won't be responsible or have to do a single mean thing except lead my mum to the *Aquarius*! Of course I don't want to hurt her (and I mean my mum), but it's much better that she knows about Mick now, before their relationship gets too serious. This is called being cruel to be kind. No wonder the man is a commitment-phobe! The revelation transforms my nausea into giddy euphoria. There's a light at the end of every tunnel – only this time it isn't a train.

'I've heard so much about the *Aquarius*, where exactly is it?' I casually ask Billy without even consciously deciding to. My mind is lucid and I'm suddenly brimming with take-charge courage.

Billy glances at me and then drops his eyes to stare balefully at my still-full glass of Pineapple Blast. He takes his work very seriously. I quickly glug a gruesome sip.

'Just around the corner,' he replies.

OK, so I'm going to need a little more than that. I stare at him hopefully. Silence. I take a second gruesome sip.

'On Belladonna Boulevard,' he adds. That's all I need to know. I grin and shove the murky drink away from me. I doubt the *Aquarius* is my sort of hangout but a girl's got to do what she's got to do. But first I must wait for Mum. I deposit three pound coins on the counter, dismount from my stool and fly down the sweep of silver steps. Mum and Lotus enter, just as I'm about to exit the building. They both have blobs of white cotton wool taped to the crook of their arms.

'Hi!' I greet them breathlessly.

'Hi,' Mum and Lotus croon in unison. They're both surprised by my apparent dazzling mood.

'How was your afternoon?' Mum asks, leaning in for a kiss.

I quickly dodge her advances and make a grab for their hands, ready to haul them in the other direction. 'Yeah fine. Now come on. I have to show you something.'

'What?' Mum laughs, which sparks a sudden flare of guilt in my chest. This is going to hurt her. Still, the alternative is far worse – for both of us.

The air outside is cold and damp and quickly settles into our skins. I'd better get moving if I'm going to hold their attention in these conditions. Turning left will take us to the beach front so I can only guess that 'around the corner' is the corner to our right. We take the first turn, which leads us to Starling Avenue.

'Did you find the book you were after?' Lotus asks, huffing to keep up.

Starling Avenue is not very long; I can see a T-Junction up ahead. I only hope that's Belladonna Boulevard.

'Libby,' Mum shakes her head at me, 'what is up with you today?'

'Er, nothing. Book? No.'

'Aurora is parked in precisely the opposite direction, you know,' Lotus exhales. Something tells me she's not enjoying the speed walk.

'It's not far to go,' I croon reassuringly.

'What's not far?' Mum laughs again. This is not a nice sort of surprise, I want to warn her but find myself unable to. She'll only start interrogating me and this is something she'll have to see to believe.

We reach the T-junction and a large signpost that says Belladonna Boulevard. Now which way? The buildings down the road to our left look like they might be concrete flats – I think I spy a beach towel hanging out of an open window and snapping in the breeze.

'We turn right again,' I instruct.

Mum's face is starting to crease with vague irritation; she hates secrets. 'Where *are* we going Liberty?' she puffs, rolling her hips to keep up with me.

I only have a few moments of their patience left. And there it is: an open door with a sign above it that says *The Age of Aquarius*. This must be it! I poke my head inside; the ground disappears immediately down a steep flight of stairs.

'Come on, this way,' I order, determinedly keeping face forward. I hear Lotus protesting something to Mum but I don't dare stop. They're both still trailing me so Mum obviously trusts me with this moment.

Our descent is brightened by intermittent naked light bulbs of different colours. As we move down deeper into the earth we're washed with red, yellow and then blue light. The stairs finally flatten out into a warm orange glow that saturates the bare brick walls dressed in posters printed with the words STAND-UP FOR PEACE. At *End War Now* we do a little more than just stand up for it, my thoughts sigh snootily. I can hear people talking and laughing not too far away. Mick must be one of them and I start stalking the sound like a tracker on a scent. Lotus and Mum are still in tow.

The orange corridor finally opens up to a very large room that's empty enough for me to see everything and everyone quite clearly. I scan the bodies; no Mick. He *must* be here! I zigzag through the clusters of loitering men and woman who are clutching drinks and swaying to more of that space age music. I know it's only a matter of seconds before Mum finally loses her patience with me. And there he is! Mick and his long satin evening dress are right in front of us. I charge up to him and point my finger, and then quickly retract it. There's no need to be cruel about this.

'See – Mick!' I burble in Mum's general direction. Her

face is completely expressionless. 'And he wears women's clothing when you're not around,' I add, just so that she's absolutely clear about what is taking place here. Mum glances from Mick to me, from me to Mick, but still she doesn't say anything. 'So what do you think?' I splutter. 'It must be a shock, but you have the right to know.' I wish she'd say something.

'Well Mick,' Mum begins, speaking calmly, 'what do you have to say for yourself?' So she's giving him a chance to defend himself. That's only fair.

Mick solidifies. He doesn't budge a muscle except for those around his eyes, which are flicking nervously between Lotus, Mum and me. Does he really think that if he stands still long enough we'll forget he's there?

'Er...sorry?' he finally offers in a high pitched voice that sounds like it came with his outfit.

'*Sorry?*' Mum reacts indignantly. I think she's finally getting into the swing of things. 'Just what do you think this is?'

Mick still hasn't shifted. He has the look of a game show contestant who is contemplating all the possible answers and desperately hoping he'll pick the right one.

'Um...the *Aquarius?*' he guesses nervously.

Mum looks disappointed and angry and hurt all at the same time. 'I thought you were better than this!'

'You did?'

'Oh yes, you bet I did!'

Lotus chooses this moment to turn away from the scene; she obviously feels embarrassed and sorry for Mick. I must admit, this isn't easy to watch.

'How could you?' Mum continues. 'I just can't believe that you would go out in public dressed like this. You…you…you *haven't even accessorised!*'

Yes Mick, you haven't even…WHAT?! 'Accessorised?' I yap out loud.

'Exactly!' Mum confirms. 'Who in their right mind steps out in a silk evening gown and doesn't bother with pearls or a diamond brooch, at the very least? And what about a clutch bag? This outfit is crying out for something in silver or gold. You're letting yourself go, Mick – that's all I really have to say on the matter.' Mum hangs her hands on her hips and shakes her head tragically. Finally Lotus turns around again. Her eyes are watering and the corners of her mouth are wrapped around her ears.

'Oh right!' Mick snorts. His face breaks wide open with sheer relief. A joke – he gets it.

'You knew?' I swallow nervously. Either there's a very logical explanation for Mick's satin get-up or my mum is into blokes who dress up in women's clothing. Either way, I'm in a whole heap of trouble.

Lotus is now making sounds like a train tooting. 'I think I may just keel over with laughter,' she hoots hysterically, 'and the show hasn't even begun yet!'

The show? Mum turns slowly to face me. Her hands are still on her hips and although her mouth is smiling her eyes certainly aren't. I know this look; she's too annoyed to let go in public. I've done it this time and she's saving herself for when we get home.

'Ah yes. The show,' Mum repeats carefully. 'Stand-Up for Peace is an annual comedy show to raise funds for *End War Now*.'

'You know, as in stand-up comedy,' Lotus fills in the blanks.

'And Mick and Layla are a comedy duo,' Mum concludes.

'Ah right, so she thought I had a thing for women's clothing,' Mick muses thoughtfully to himself. He's building a jigsaw puzzle and just about has all the pieces.

I hear everything they're saying but still my brain won't absorb it, because when it does I'll have to accept a bunch of other things too – like the fact that I have just made a complete fool of myself in front of everyone (again); that my plan has backfired, making Mick the helpless victim and me the potty pest (I'm seeing a pattern); and that all I've succeeded in doing is pushing Mum even closer to her boyfriend (it's like déjà vu). Why is it that whenever things start going my way it's usually because I'm in the wrong freaking lane!

'You know, I think I'll make the comedy show after all,' Mum announces resolutely. 'I'll just drop Libby off at home first.'

Mick and Lotus both nod in reply and stare at me pitifully. Mum is staring at me too. And nobody is laughing any more. Now I really feel like an outsider. Why is it that no one is paying attention until you make a mistake?

nineteen
the dream team

Neither of us uttered a single word during the drive home. Mum gripped the steering wheel fiercely and stared holes into the road ahead, while I peered nervously out at the scenery whizzing past the passenger window. My actions seem pathetic and ridiculous now. But worse yet, I think Mum is going off me. Something tells me I'm not the light of her life any more.

When we get home she heads straight for her bedroom and plonks herself down in front of her dressing table, where she begins madly brushing her goose-down head. I follow and rest my shoulder against the bedroom door frame and silently watch her brushing. One or two quick sweeps of a comb would have done it; her short white hair is now surging with static electricity. She clucks in irritation and reaches for a tub of gel which she applies to her head with dextrous fingertips. This soothes her hair, making it drift down to her scalp in soft, shiny wisps.

'I'm sorry Mum,' I finally speak.

She doesn't answer immediately and focuses her

attention on a small pot of silky powder instead. Using a small brush she hastily applies some of the pale powder to her eyelids. She then stares into the mirror, blinking her silky lids over pupils that are small and pointed with anger.

'I just don't understand you Libby.' She eventually responds in a voice that's hard and snappy. 'Don't you want me to be happy, is that it?'

My talking thoughts want desperately to explain that I do want her to be happy, but I want me to be happy too. And being happy means being with her again. Otherwise I'm doomed.

'Of course I do,' I reply simply.

'Mick's a good man, he doesn't deserve this.'

There we go, back to Mick again. This isn't really even about him – not personally anyway.

'I didn't say he wasn't a good man. I uh…just thought he was a transvestite, that's all. What was I supposed to think?' My opinions may have changed but not the fact that I'm right. Sort of.

'And what about the scene you created at *Green Leaves*?' Mum challenges. 'I'm trying to be patient with you Liberty, but you're making it very difficult.' She swaps the powder for her mascara wand and begins manically stroking her eyelashes. It looks dangerous.

'I'm not even asking you to be especially nice to Mick. All I expect is for you not to be rude to him. Is that too much to ask?'

'Nope,' I gulp miserably. My throat has constricted and my eyes are burning. She's disappointed in me for not fitting in better.

'Tonight is a really big deal, but I decided not to go to the comedy show. I decided to stay at home with you instead because I could see you were struggling to come to terms with my relationship with Mick. But after your performance today I think I should go. I think I owe it to Mick.' Now she's got a pale pink lipstick in her hand and is rolling the shimmering colour on her lips.

I'm not going to beg my own mother to stay at home with me. 'Don't think I'm bothered!' I retaliate angrily. I can't seem to dodge the landmines so I might as well stomp right through them. 'And if you think I could care less about your stupid relationship with Mick then you're wrong there too. You think your new life in Brighton is so special and brilliant? Well I have a life too. And a family that includes a brother. And we're also happy. So you can have Mick and your stupid Kooky Centre, because it makes zero difference to me!' That will have to be my parting statement because my head has suddenly filled up with water. I turn from her bedroom door and stride down the passage to the bathroom, where I slam the door and lock it tight behind me. Now what? My nose is burning and wet and my eyes are dripping firewater. I shove the plug in the bathtub and turn both taps on full, adding a steady stream of bubble bath to the gush of hot water. I'm already in the tub and peering through bubbles when Mum knocks on the door.

'Libby, I think we need to talk.' I don't breathe a word. The silent treatment sends my mother crazy – a favourite hobby of my father's but not a great talent of mine, unfortunately. My emotions don't have a control panel.

'Just go to the freaking comedy show,' I shout. 'I want to be alone!' That was my silent treatment then.

Mum remains standing outside the bathroom door for a while before I hear her footsteps walking away. Now there's a shuffling sound coming from the living room. Then the front door opens and closes again. A car starts up and drives away. If I wasn't trying very hard to be optimistic I'd say that it sounded exactly like Aurora. And now there's only silence and the drip-drip of the bath tap. So much for optimism then. She gave up on me so easily.

When the doorbell rings I've been in the bath long enough for the pale pads of my fingertips and toes to transform into pickled onions. I contemplate ignoring the door but the bathwater has also turned cool on me. I'm also completely bored with my self-pity.

Ding-dong.

I climb into Mum's fluffy white terrycloth robe and splat wet feet in the direction of the front door. The too-big robe is trailing behind me like a bridal gown. Like a bride that's been ditched at the altar, more like it. I am feeling so sorry for myself.

Ding-dong. These New Agers are impatient. I open the door. It's Sam.

'Oh, hello,' I greet him with surprise. 'What are you doing here?'

'Nice to see you too, Liberty Belle. Mind if I come inside?'

'Uh, sure.' I immediately step back from the door. 'I was uh…just in the bath,' I add, pulling the robe tighter to me.

'Yes, I can tell. Best you go get dressed then.'

'I'll only be a minute.' I shut the door behind him and swoosh toward the dining room where I rummage in my suitcase for some clean clothes to ferry over to the bathroom. When I finally emerge Sam is paging through the latest edition of *Serenity Weekly* magazine.

'How did you know I was home?' I ask.

'Your mum phoned and offered to fetch and drop me off here.'

So I'm a charity case then! 'I'm perfectly all right on my own,' I snap.

'Nobody said you weren't, but I was also sitting at home on my own so your mum figured we might as well hang out together. Gloria has gone to the Stand-Up Comedy Fundraiser, she was really excited too.'

Stand-Up la-la whatever, my thoughts bristle. I was planning on working on my Last Will and Testament this evening; instinct tells me that I don't have much time left and I still have so much to plan and organise before I die. I've got to write Mum a letter too – clearing things up and telling her how I feel, just in case I don't get the chance to explain in person. I don't want her spending the rest of her life thinking bad thoughts about me. Still, I suppose I can hang out with Sam for one night. 'Can we please just not talk about parents, at least,' I plead, 'because I'm putting myself up for adoption. Can you do that – nominate yourself? Who cares, because I am.'

'You shouldn't talk like that.'

'Oh, whatever,' I conclude, because this is the place in the conversation where I've grown tired of talking about all this hooey.

'How about we make a stack of pancakes?' Sam suggests. 'I'm an ace with a saucepan and whisk.'

'I suppose.' I lead him in the direction of the kitchen. 'I should warn you though, my cooking is even worse than my skills with the flower sticks.'

'Oh right. Well best you stay over there then.' He points to an area of the kitchen where I'll be well out the way. I do as I'm told and watch as he searches the cupboards for the ingredients and implements he'll need to make this stack of pancakes he's been bragging about.

'So are you still taking control of your happiness then?' he asks when he finally has all the necessaries spread out across the kitchen counter.

'Ah, not so much,' I sigh dismissively. 'I think I've given up on it, to be honest.'

'That's a shame.'

'Yeah well, there are certain things you cannot control.' Like Mum and Mick moving in together.

Sam changes the subject to update me on the *End War Now* peaceful protest march which is scheduled for just a few days' time. He tells me that some protesters like to dress up and wear masks to symbolise the terror of war. I reply that Mum and I will definitely be going along but I doubt whether I'll bother with a scary mask. Sam agrees and doesn't think he will either.

The smell of sizzling pancakes is belly rumbling and strangely comforting. Mum used to make pancakes for breakfast whenever it was one of our birthdays. Even my father's. He wouldn't eat them any other time though; he called them empty calories.

'Here you go, have a bite of this.' Sam approaches me with a rolled up pancake dripping with lemon juice and cinnamon sugar. The pancake zones in on my mouth and I don't have time to protest – I can either open up for the pancake train or have it mushed against my pressed lips. It tastes delicious. 'So what do you think?'

'Absolutely yummy!' I applaud. Sam finishes the other half of the pancake and licks the sweetness from his fingertips appreciatively.

'Yes, I do have a remarkable talent,' he grins.

'And you're so modest,' I laugh. Thanks to Sam I've once again almost entirely forgotten my troubles. He feels like a best friend.

'Hold on a minute,' he says, suddenly moving in closer towards me with his eyes narrowed in concentration. 'You have something on your...' He then leans forward and presses his lips gently against my own.

I'm so shocked I don't move, but I can feel and smell and his lips are soft and full and his scent still reminds me of Christmas spice. I close my eyes and breathe in deeply. The tip of his nose tickles my own – a reminder of our closeness. Everything I ever knew or recognised as Sam has intensified a thousand times over, making him shiny and new like the first day we met. I'd imagined our kiss beforehand, but this is way more than anything I could have dreamt up. When Sam finally pulls away and I open my eyes again he's staring straight at me. His differently coloured eyes are twice as beautiful.

'Sorry, you had a bit of syrup on your lip,' he smiles apologetically.

'That pancake had cinnamon sugar and lemon on it. No syrup,' I beam back mischievously.

'Oh right,' Sam nods, looking perplexed, 'that is strange. I must be mistaken. I'd better double-check.' He then leans forward for the second time in as many minutes. Only this time I'm a little more prepared and our next kiss is even more sweet and spectacular than the first.

twenty
a sea of plenty

Gloria and Sam's house is a blur of busy excitement. Today is the day of the big protest march and the New Age *End War Now* campaigners are arriving in their blended rainbow-tone droves. I haven't seen many scary masks about the place yet, although many of the protesters will be joining the march as it weaves its way through the streets of Brighton. They're expecting quite a turn out and Sam and I have been working hard at putting the finishing daubs to the last few banners. And we're almost done.

'Hey, I've got an idea,' a strange voice suddenly speaks from above.

Sam and I are both on all fours and trying not to kneel in paint. We carefully twist to face the voice. There's a man with long curly hair wrapped in a paisley bandanna staring down at us.

Sam surveys the man dubiously. 'You do?'

'Sure. Instead of the banner saying GIVE PEACE A CHANCE, how about you make one that says GIVE PEAS A CHANCE?'

'Huh?' Sam and I yelp in unison.

'I'm general secretary of the Vegetarian Society,' the man reveals with a sheepish shrug of his shoulders, 'and we could really do with the publicity. Can't hurt, can it?' he adds optimistically.

'Well no,' Sam agrees, 'but we've already finished making the signs – this was the last one.'

'Ah right. Well it was worth a mention.'

Mmm, someone's collided with their wind chimes once too often, my talking thoughts grin at Sam. My right hand is touching his left hand but to anyone looking on this could seem incidental and unimportant. I really fancy Sam, but I don't want my mum to find out. Or Gloria. Or anyone else, for that matter. Not yet.

'How are you guys getting on?' That's my mum's voice and she's standing where the general secretary of the Vegetarian Society was just a short while ago. I move my right hand to scratch my head.

'Uh, just fine – we're done in fact,' I reply nonchalantly. Mum and I both said sorry and agreed to sit and talk it out soon, but things are still a little weird at the moment.

'Oh good, great job.'

'Thanks.'

'We're about to get the show on the road. Perhaps you

should go to the loo before we head off Libby, there won't be any along the way,' she suggests, like I'm prone to wetting my pants when not regularly reminded to go to the toilet. Could my mother be any more embarrassing?

'I'm fine,' I growl and busy myself with packing away the pots of paint.

'Suit yourself, but don't come crying to me when you're bursting and have to squat in a bush.'

THANK YOU MOTHER! She turns and disappears down the corridor, calling out for Gloria while I turn away from Sam and pray for my cheeks to fade. Suddenly she's an expert on my bladder! I wonder how I manage to get by when she's not around, my talking thoughts scowl.

'Mums—!' Sam chuckles. 'Come on, this one will be ours.' He rolls the banner up and I follow him outside where clusters of peace-lovers are milling about the pavement looking eager to get started. We wait for Mum and Gloria and then join their ranks and slowly shuffle forward with our painted protests held high and our spirits even higher. I'm tripping over my feet in excitement; we're going to bring peace to all mankind! If nothing else, at least I will do something worthwhile before I die.

Today must be one of the hottest days so far and it's

not long before my skin turns slippery and my hair fuses to the nape of my neck. But the heat doesn't put anyone off and as we proceed toward the beach front, groups of protesters of all types join our parade. Some have banners while others have masks that look faintly tribal with jagged teeth and colourful war paint. One protester has gone a step further and is dressed in a business suit with a rubber facemask that looks like the bloke on telly my father enjoys referring to as 'our Slime Minister'.

The man with sweaty patches and lamb chop sideburns marching in front of me has made an enormous peace sign out of papier mâché and attached it to the end of a pole. He's walking along and waving it happily in the air like a giant lollipop. A woman waving a fistful of lit incense sticks joins the procession and begins swaying and dancing to the music in her head. The general mood is one of friendship and solidarity; we're all members of the same happy family.

With our numbers swelling and our moods soaring, pedestrians and bypassers stop and stare and take photos. One onlooker has even climbed up a tree to get a better view. My heart billows in my chest; I feel so proud. As we near the town centre, policemen in helmets cradling batons suddenly step out from the shadows. They've obviously been waiting for our arrival.

'They're just precautionary,' Mum assures me, 'this is a peaceful protest.' Sure, but they definitely add to the excitement! Sam looks just as keyed up and gives me a subtle grin and a wink. I grin back but I don't wink; I could never be that cool.

'Where's Mick?' I hear Gloria ask my mum.

'I'm not sure,' she replies, 'he said he'd join us at the corner of Pritchard Avenue. Perhaps he's been held up; there are an awful lot of people here today.' She's trying to sound casual, but I can see her scanning the crowds anxiously in search of him. I pretend I haven't heard a thing and try to focus on something else – like the fact that I need the toilet, instead. But that's not something to focus on. That's another thing for me to ignore.

'Where exactly are we walking to?' I change the subject and ask Sam.

'We're heading for the Mayor of Brighton's office, where *End War Now* will present him with a signed petition protesting violence and war.'

Oh right. I wonder if he'd mind if I use his loo?

Eventually the protesters in the lead start slowing and the peace-lovers at the back start pooling around them. Everyone is lingering and chatting and looking expectant, so I think one of the buildings nearby must be the Mayor's spot. Mum is still scanning the crowds while my bladder weighs heavy like a shotput in my stomach.

'So who exactly presents the Mayor with the petition?' I ask Sam, desperate to divert my thoughts.

'I don't know,' he replies and raises his eyebrows, like it'll be interesting to see just exactly who gets to scale the government steps armed with a whole bunch of signatures. A woman with flowers in her hair has mounted a low wall and is twirling a baton for the crowds, while a group of woolly students write messages like 'Peace is our only hope' in chalk on the pavement and street. The baton lady is growing more confident and suddenly begins shouting out a chant.

'One, two, three, four, we want an end to war!' she hollers.

A few enthusiastic peace-lovers start joining in, which brings confidence to those less outspoken and before we know it just about everyone is chanting and wagging their fists in the air. I never thought the day would come when I'd be shouting protests outside the Mayor's office, but at this very moment in time it feels as though it was something I was born to do – as if my destiny has finally been fulfilled. Right now I think I'd do just about anything for my fellow protesters. I'd do it for the cause, and because we're like family. I grin at

Sam and get my fist-wagging in sync with his. He grins back at me and nudges me gently with his non-protesting elbow. The heat has turned his temples blistered and shiny.

I'm not exactly sure what takes place next, it all happens so quickly the pictures run into one another like a psychedelic smudge. I can only recall flashes of images, like snapshots from a camera set on a timer. First two men appear dressed in soldier's desert-tan uniforms with matching bush hats and black leather combat boots. They've painted their faces like bright clowns and are rolling to the rhythm of the chant. I see them coming, but Sam doesn't. He swings around when they're practically on top of him. And then he's on the floor, writhing and shaking and fighting for breath with eyes that are white and bulging grotesquely out of their sockets. His shirt is sweat-soaked in an instant and there's a dark wet patch spreading across the crotch of his cargo shorts. He jerks his legs up and his heels scrape frantically at the tar, as if he's scrambling to escape from an encroaching terror.

The next thing I see is Gloria on the ground beside him with one hand pushing at his forehead and the other weighing on his heaving belly. She's calm and in control and calling out to him in soothing tones. She's telling him over and over that he's OK, but still his face remains contorted with acute fear and helplessness. The two clown soldiers look alarmed and try to help, but Mum steps in and pushes them back. Then, suddenly, Mick is there and on the floor beside Gloria. He raises Sam off the hot tar and presses his shaking body to him. He has a bottle in his hand and is crooning and trickling water over my friend's burning head. Mick and Gloria both lean in close and use their bodies to shield Sam from the faces of the panicky crowd. They're both reminding him who they are and assuring him that he's safe. I'm standing there uselessly, whilst saying a prayer over and over in my head. Please don't let Sam die. Please don't let Sam die. I'm the one who's meant to die, remember?

'Could you all step back,' I hear Mum pleading.

I want to be with Sam but I'm scared of what's happening to him, so just like my large extended family, I do as she says. When Gloria and Mick finally break, my next image is of a slightly calmer Sam just managing to sit upright. His thick black curls are tousled and contrast with his face which is as pale and dull as limestone. But he's breathing normally and he seems to recognise who we are and where he is. There's talk of ambulances and hospital but Gloria dismisses the offers with her hand raised firmly in the air. 'Thank you for your concern,' she says to the faces of strangers staring intently, 'but he's all right. We just need to get him home.'

Like some divine intervention the jostling crowds suddenly part, creating a clear path for us to walk through. Mick has Sam by one armpit and Gloria has him by the other, and together they manoeuvre him away from the horde of peace-lovers. Mum takes my hand and I wrap my trembling fingers gratefully around hers. I still have no idea what just took place here but seeing to Sam is more important right now than asking.

'I'm not parked far from here,' Mick says. 'You wait and I'll be back in a moment.' Quiet, bumbling Mick has been usurped by a quick-thinking, take-charge kind of guy. They settle Sam on the grass beneath the shade of a tree and he leans back with his eyes closed. His breathing is normal and his hand is pressed against his forehead.

'Do you have a headache?' Gloria asks. He nods slowly. 'I'll give you tablets as soon as we get home,' she calms him.

Mick is true to his word and reappears behind the wheel of his battered car a short while later. He leaves the engine running and they have Sam loaded up in no time.

'I'll call you, Iris,' Gloria smiles wanly.

Mum launches a kiss off the flat of her palm and into the air. 'It will all be OK,' she reassures her friend with a confident nod of her white head. I don't know how she can be so sure.

twenty-one
you can't always run

Mum drove us home and kept us busy with small talk about Aurora's cranky gearshift and the sluggish Brighton traffic while I stared blankly out of the car windscreen, lightly stippled with sharp salt air. So much for rush hour, the traffic moved slower than ever. Not that I could have cared less, there was nowhere I really wanted to be.

Now that we're home Mum is fussing over a pitcher of yellow lemon wedges bobbing along on a sea of iced tea which ripples with fresh mint leaves.

'Let's go and sit in the garden,' she suggests. She doesn't wait for my RSVP and immediately carries the pitcher and two glasses out of the kitchen door through to the green wrought-iron chairs and table nestling on the unmown patch of lawn dotted with daisies at the back of the small, lopsided cottage. She's stalling and obviously needs a run up to this discussion.

'I suppose you're wondering what happened to your friend Sam today,' she eventually begins, handing me a tall glass of cold tea with things floating in it.

I accept the drink and silently hold on to it like a lifebuoy. That wasn't a question and I don't want to disrupt her flow. She runs a hand over her goose head and puckers her face in concentration. 'Where do I begin?' she asks herself. 'Well, Sam is actually Samir Pejic. Or that's the name he was given at birth, anyway. He was born in Bosnia, which is properly known as Bosnia-Herzegovina, which was once a state in communist Yugoslavia before it sought independence and…'

'I know there was a war in Bosnia,' I interrupt her. So I have a vague idea, but I'm more desperate for news expressly about Sam, or this stranger called Samir Pejic.

'Gloria had a son and he was called Adam,' Mum continues. 'About ten years ago – when Adam was nineteen years old – he was sent to Bosnia with the United Nations peacekeeping forces. And one day the humanitarian convoy he was leading into the capital Sarajevo was hit by a mortar shell. Adam was killed, along with three others.' Mum pauses and suddenly looks drawn and sombre. I also take a moment to think about Gloria and how she must have felt when she heard that her brave son – the peacekeeper leading the humanitarian convoy – was dead. He was so far away from home.

'Gloria, understandably, took the news very badly.' Mum resumes the story. 'She was a single mum and Adam was her only child. She had basically just lost her entire family and for a while she was very low and rather bitter, not only for the loss of her own son, but for the suffering of so many people caught up in the tragedy of the war in Bosnia. But after a while she grew stronger and decided to turn her grief inside out. She wanted something good to come from Adam's death. And that was how we came to know Sam, or Samir Pejic. He's a Bosnian war orphan and Gloria legally adopted him and brought him back to live with her in England when he was only four years old.'

'What happened to Sam's family?' I ask.

Mum jiggles her glass and stares at a lemon wedge riding the iced tea waves. 'Sam saw what no child should ever see, Libby,' she finally speaks. 'His family was killed right in front of him. He was very young and perhaps that's why he was allowed to live, but he was the only one of his family who survived.' She doesn't add anything further and swallows her sadness with a long sip of her drink.

'Does Sam remember his family, and how they died?' I whisper.

'Oh, he remembers small things about them – like his mum's songs and his older brother's passion for juggling anything that wasn't nailed down. And yes, unfortunately he remembers small fragments of the day they were killed. He's had counselling and worked through some of the memories and the pain of his loss. He used to have terrible nightmares – they call it Post Traumatic Stress Disorder. But he now seems to have made some peace with his past. And Gloria and Sam are a family; they've helped each other to heal. But they'll never quite forget. Perhaps seeing those men in soldiers' uniforms with painted faces confused and scared Sam. I don't suppose the heat and the crowds and the noise of today helped much either. I think it was all just too much for him. He's had panic attacks before, and this probably won't be the last of them either. But he'll be just fine, I promise.'

Sam has always seemed so steady and normal and it's taking me a while to make sense of this Samir Pejic. I gaze down the road our friendship has taken, looking for signs pointing to the real Sam along the way. There's almost nothing. I once asked him about his dad, I reminisce guiltily. He simply said that it had been a very long time since he'd seen him. If only I'd known I'd have kept my gigantic trap shut tight. Poor poor Sam.

And what about poor poor Adam; it was his death that brought my friend to England. Who knows what would have happened to Sam otherwise. I remember the first day I ever visited Sam and Gloria's house – the day Mick slapped my mother's rump and I passed spaghetti through my nose. There was a photo of a young man in a soldier's uniform on the bureau in their lounge. That must have been Adam.

Nestled in my mum's overgrown back garden I sit and contemplate this thing called life. I've been so preoccupied with dying I haven't really given it a moment's thought. All the small choices we make carry us in a certain direction. That's our destiny. But it's a self-made destiny, one that we create for ourselves and shape with our desires and determination. Everything we think, say or do has an effect on our future and the happiness or unhappiness of those around us, because we're all eddies of the same whirlpool. But we won't always understand life, or the direction in which we're swirling. And every now and again some good might just mould itself out of something that seems so bad at the time. Who knows, maybe one day I'll look back and see things differently and understand what happened to my own family too. Maybe it has to do with the adult I've yet to grow into.

'It's been said,' Mum finally speaks again, 'that for a parent to outlive their child is the worst kind of grief.' She looks up from her glass to me with eyes that are soaked in tears. 'You're so precious to me, Liberty Belle, we really should never ever argue.' The wetness rolls down her cheeks like raindrops and her shoulders surrender and slump forward sadly. My stand-tall, cheerful Mum – I'm surprised to discover, is lost too. Maybe this hasn't been any easier for her after all.

I don't go to her immediately; my talking thoughts need time to think. I don't know when I first decided that death was waiting for me just around the corner. I couldn't say what brought it on. But I do know that saying goodbye to my mum is the thing I fear most in this world. And thinking about it, I suppose in a way death is like the ultimate goodbye. Has my fear overtaken me? I glance up at Mum, who looks bewildered. She doesn't know why it all went wrong either, but if I died she'd definitely be the saddest person alive. Because even though my parents are divorced and my mum lives far away, I'm still her baby girl. I haven't lost my family entirely. Like Sam and Gloria, we're simply a different sort of family now. Maybe this isn't the end of my world. Like Samir, perhaps it's not my time to die after all.

My eyes are awake but the rest of me won't hear of it. I focus on the laser beams of white light slanting in through the blinds above me in the dining room of the lopsided cottage at the seaside. If I concentrate hard enough their warmth might melt the icy fear that's frozen my veins. I try to move my limbs but my joints are strained and rigid. It's like I'm being pulled in opposite directions on a medieval stretching rack instead of napping on a futon. I know what this is, I'm having another one. I'm paralysed in my sleep again. My mind is alert but I've lost all contact with the rest of me. Houston, I think we have a problem. If I could just lift my head up…but there's a crushing weight bearing down on me. I'm starting to panic when suddenly the door opens and Lotus is looming over me.

'You awake?' she whispers. Her familiar voice washes over me and dissolves the rush of panic that overpowered and pinned me down when I wasn't looking.

'Uh, yeh,' I blink nervously and swivel my neck and

elbows like Pinocchio set free from his puppet strings.

'It's your father,' she says and holds out the cordless phone. I stare at the plastic ivory handset dangling in front of me and try to make sense of the news. Ah right, she means it's my father calling. I accept the phone and scrape my voice against my throat to clear it.

'Ahem, hello?'

'Hello Liberty, it's your father calling.' Thanks for clearing that up, my talking thoughts grumble tiredly. 'So how have you enjoyed your holiday in Brighton?' he asks with his own brand of stiff enthusiasm.

Reality hits me like a sledgehammer. That's right, today is my last day with Mum and Sam and the rest of my friends in Brighton. School starts on Monday and I've got to race back to my life in Manchester and pick up where I left off. This past week has pulled across my eyes in a blur. Mum took a few days off from the Kooky Centre and we spent the time walking along the beach and talking and dancing to old Eighties songs and watching girly movies with hooked pinkie fingers. I even showed her my remembrance collage for Tommy, although I didn't call it that – just in case I don't have to die after all. She absolutely loved the Gustav Klimt postcard and said it reminded her of us when I was that small. I wanted to say that this was exactly why I liked the postcard too, but I didn't because I knew that if I said the words I would cry. And I have to be careful and try very hard not to cry when the time to say goodbye is close by. Once I start crying, I find it very difficult to stop.

'Liberty?'

Oh yes, my father...my holiday. 'Uh fine,' I murmur and then remember that I shouldn't sound sad or my father will get in a strop. 'I've had fun,' I add with fake cheeriness.

'Well that's good then,' he adds, like that's one more thing out of the way. 'Sophie called wanting to know when you were coming home.'

Ah right, home. I am home. 'She did?' It's all I can manage in response to rollercoaster Sophie.

'Yes. I told her that you were arriving tonight and that she could call you on Sunday if she wished, although I think we should have a family day on Sunday – you know, and maybe do something together before you go back to school. Your school blazer is dry-cleaned, so you're ready to go.'

'Thanks.'

'Misty is still very tired but she can manage an outing. How about we take Thomas to the zoo?' he suggests.

'OK great,' I sigh. It's not that I have anything

against taking Tommy to the zoo, but right now my brain can't move past saying goodbye to Mum. And I don't want to waste precious time thinking about my starchy existence in Manchester; I still need a bit more of Mum and Sam's carefree passion and spirit. I've barely seen Sam this week; he spent a lot of time at home sleeping. Yesterday we all went to a boat race though. We ate smoked cockles and laughed loudly and slapped our thighs like we'd never even been apart. I told him that I knew about his past and he nodded and said he was glad that I did. He didn't even seem embarrassed that I had seen him wet his pants, but that's because he knows that I care and think he's brilliant and would never judge him. He knows it because I told him.

'So I'll see you at the station then?' my father says, reeling the conversation in.

'Yes. Great. Thanks. See you then. Bye.' I wait for his parting 'goodbye' and press the red button on the phone. Lotus left the room long ago.

We're having a sit-down farewell lunch together – Mum, me, Mick, Lotus, Gloria and Sam, and I can hear pots rattling and cupboards banging. *Reincarnation for Believers* is on the floor near my feet and I scoop it up and remove the slips of paper trapped between the pages. My notes to Mum – I've still got to hide them. I think I'll leave the first one in her jewellery box. It's the Gustav Klimt postcard; Tommy won't mind.

While Mum and Lotus finish preparing lunch I pack my bags and search in sheltered places for things I might have forgotten. It's better to keep busy. I couldn't say in what order things happened after that. Mick, Gloria and Sam arrived and we chatted and ate. Or ate and chatted, I'm really not quite sure. I was nice to Mick, I made certain of that. Not just for Mum's sake, but because he's a good guy. Somewhere along the way Lotus gave me a copy of Oscar Wilde's *The Happy Prince* which she'd found in a second-hand bookshop. And then suddenly it was my time to leave.

Mick carried my bags to Aurora and kissed me on my cheek. It didn't weird me out either. Gloria hugged me and I looked her in the eyes to let her know that I knew about Adam and that I was sorry about what had happened. And then Lotus came along and held me tight and rubbed my back and told me to be good and take even better care. And then Mum, Sam and I climbed into Aurora and rattled down the road to the station. That's sort of how I remember it.

Now Sam and I are standing on the station platform and looking awkward while Mum has disappeared to check about an open annual train ticket. He's holding a brown paper bag in his hand.

'I'm really going to miss you, Liberty Belle,' he says. His mouth pulls with a smile but it's the straight, hard kind that just sits there without spreading.

'I'm going to miss you so much too, Sam. You're the best friend I've ever had.'

'What, as in a spot-the-difference boy type of friend?' he grins. This time it reaches his eyes.

'Maybe more,' I smile shyly. 'You'd better wait for my next visit to find out.'

'I won't have to wait too long, I hope,' he says sadly.

'Not too long,' I confirm just as a big fat tear tumbles down my cheek.

'This is for you,' he changes the subject and shoves the brown bag at me.

I take a look inside, it's one of his mirrors decorated with shells and driftwood. 'Thank you Sam, I'll treasure it.' I swallow hard and concentrate on breathing. Just then Mum appears and the first whistle blows.

'Right, it's organised,' she chimes with wild, panicked eyes. 'I'll let you know when you can collect the ticket, Lib.'

'OK,' I choke. The second whistle shrieks. I've got to get on the train now.

''Bye Libby, take care of yourself,' Sam says and locks his arms around me. He still smells like Christmas spice. I don't reply. I can't. But I hug him back tightly so that he knows everything I'm feeling right now. He then steps back quickly and makes room for my mum, who pulls me against her and winds her arms tenderly around my head. I can't help it – if I don't cry I'll explode, and the tears fall so hard they make my shoulders shake. I grab a handful of Mum's muslin top and try to memorise all her details – like her smell, what she feels like and the heat of her skin as it rubs hotly against my cheek which is burning with the salt from my weeping.

'I'll see you very soon, Libby,' she finally breathes, gently smoothing her hand over and over my head. The third whistle blows and she has to prise me off her chest. Her face meets mine and her sad eyes search my own. Her cheeks are mottled and greasy.

'I love you,' she says.

The next thing I know I'm inside the train and staring blearily out of the half-open carriage window. Mum and Sam are still standing on the platform. The train gives one long final whistle and begins juddering.

'I'll be back soon,' I cry out and wave to Sam. I exist between two worlds. And somewhere in the middle is me.

I look at Mum and she blows me a kiss. I breathe deep and use everything I have inside me to shout the words I feel I've spent a lifetime practising. 'I love you, goodbye!'

The End

Other Orchard books you might enjoy

Utterly Me, Clarice Bean	Lauren Child	978 1 84362 304 5	£4.99
Clarice Bean Spells Trouble	Lauren Child	978 1 84362 858 3	£4.99
Ella Mental and the Good Sense Guide	Amber Deckers	978 1 84362 727 2	£5.99
Ella Mental – Life, Love and More Good Sense	Amber Deckers	978 1 84616 212 1	£5.99
Clair de Lune	Cassandra Golds	978 1 84362 926 9	£4.99
The Truth About Josie Green	Belinda Hollyer	978 1 84362 885 9	£4.99
My Scary Fairy Godmother	Rose Impey	978 1 84362 683 1	£4.99
Shooting Star	Rose Impey	978 1 84362 560 5	£4.99
Hothouse Flower	Rose Impey	978 1 84616 215 2	£4.99
Do Not Read This Book	Pat Moon	978 1 84121 435 1	£4.99
Do Not Read Any Further	Pat Moon	978 1 84121 456 6	£4.99
Do Not Read Or Else!	Pat Moon	978 1 84616 082 0	£4.99

Orchard books are available from all good bookshops, or can be ordered
direct from the publisher: Orchard Books, PO BOX 29, Douglas IM99 1BQ
Credit card orders please telephone 01624 836000 or fax 01624 837033 or
visit our internet site: www.wattspub.co.uk or e-mail:
bookshop@enterprise.net for details.

To order please quote title, author and ISBN
and your full name and address.
Cheques and postal orders should be made payable to 'Bookpost plc.'
Postage and packing is FREE within the UK
(overseas customers should add £1.00 per book).

Prices and availability are subject to change.